*Don't Wake Me Up
While I'm Driving*

By Margaret Scherf
DON'T WAKE ME UP WHILE I'M DRIVING
IF YOU WANT A MURDER WELL DONE
TO CACHE A MILLIONAIRE
THE BEAUTIFUL BIRTHDAY CAKE
THE BANKER'S BONES
THE CORPSE IN THE FLANNEL NIGHTGOWN
THE DIPLOMAT AND THE GOLD PIANO
NEVER TURN YOUR BACK
JUDICIAL BODY
THE CAUTIOUS OVERSHOES
GLASS ON THE STAIRS
DEAD: SENATE OFFICE BUILDING
THE ELK AND THE EVIDENCE
THE GREEN PLAID PANTS
THE CURIOUS CUSTARD PIE
THE GUN IN DANIEL WEBSTER'S BUST
GILBERT'S LAST TOOTHACHE
MURDER MAKES ME NERVOUS
ALWAYS MURDER A FRIEND
THE OWL IN THE CELLAR

Juveniles
THE MYSTERY OF THE VELVET BOX
THE MYSTERY OF THE SHAKY STAIRCASE
THE MYSTERY OF THE EMPTY TRUNK

Don't Wake Me Up While I'm Driving

MARGARET SCHERF

PUBLISHED FOR THE CRIME CLUB BY
DOUBLEDAY AND COMPANY, INC.
GARDEN CITY, NEW YORK
1977

All of the characters in this book are fictitious, and any resemblance to actual persons, living or dead, is purely coincidental.

Library of Congress Cataloging in Publication Data

Scherf, Margaret.
Don't wake me up while I'm driving.

I. Title.
PZ3.S3263Do [PS3537.C3214]   813'.5'2
ISBN: 0-385-12253-5
Library of Congress Catalog Card Number 76–19622

Copyright © 1977 by Margaret Scherf
All Rights Reserved
Printed in the United States of America
First Edition

*Don't Wake Me Up
While I'm Driving*

1

Someone was pounding on the door. Hal tried not to hear it, pulling himself back into sleep.

The deep voice of George Finley came through. "Get up, Hal, for God's sake."

"Come in, George. The door's open."

George came in, bringing cold with him, and stamping snow from his boots. "I never thought it would happen. Nobody thought it could happen."

"What?"

"Minot is dry."

Hal sat up. "Your nose is frozen."

George paid no attention. "This is the first time since Volstead that Minot has been totally without liquor. Thirteen long, defiant years. And we're defeated not by the law, but by the weather."

Hal pulled his pillow up against the iron bedstead and uncovered a brown paper bag. He had no idea what was in it. "Has anybody got any plans?"

"No, not even Olsen. He has everything lined up for a run to Wisconsin, but nobody can get through—the drifts between here and Minneapolis are ten feet deep."

Hal opened the paper bag. It contained twelve cold tamales. "Where did I get these?"

"The other question is, Do you always sleep on your lunch?"

"I think I was drinking last night."

"You were. And so, alas, was I."

"Where did we do our drinking?"

"We started at the Prairie Dog, then we went to the Park Hotel, then out to the Red Lantern, and we wound up downstairs at Toni Murphy's Cigar Store and Speakeasy."

"It's damned cold in here. Bang on the radiator with the wrench, George."

"Why don't you move to the Park Hotel? They keep it warm."

"Rosie doesn't like the Park. Too close to being a House."

"She's a good girl, Rosie."

"If there was so much booze in town last night, what happened to it?"

"The supply was exhausted by persons like yourself and Hawkspeare and Pollywog Louis and High Ass Swede, and those rails at the Park Hotel. Shall I make some coffee?" George found the coffee and the enamel pot. He used about equal amounts of water and coffee. As he said, you didn't have to live by a river to make good coffee.

After the second cup, Hal proposed that they go up to Canada and bring back some real whiskey.

"We can't get through the snow."

"They say the road is plowed as far as Stanfield. We can shovel our way from there to Portal, maybe."

George didn't look with favor on shoveling through fifteen miles of drifts. He wanted to know where they were going to find the money for this trip. "My funds are down to four dollars and eighty-seven cents."

Hal swung his warm feet onto the cold linoleum, emptied his pants pocket. "Thirteen-fifty. That makes seventeen dollars and thirty-seven cents."

"A case is thirty-six dollars. We're a bit short."

"Barney has twenty-four dollars saved up for his wedding."

"Your brother is trusting, even gullible, but he won't let you touch that money."

"I'll double it."

"Or lose it entirely."

At that critical moment Barney arrived, looking pinched and white in his thin old coat and no gloves. He had a worried smile as he poured himself some coffee. Barney generally looked as healthy as a red apple.

"Are you sick, kid? You look pale around the gills."

"It's cold out. Forty below."

"Cold never made you look pale before. What is it?"

"Hortense and I are getting married Sunday."

"Sunday! This Sunday?" Hal saw the twenty-four dollars slipping away. "How would you like a wedding present of forty-eight dollars?"

"Look out, Barney," George warned.

"That's a lot of money. Are you sure you can spare that much?"

"Sure. Here's all you have to do. Let me borrow the twenty-four you have in the bank, and I'll more than double it in three days."

"No. I can't do that. Hortense said don't let anybody—meaning you—talk me out of that money. She'd kill me, Hal."

"She won't be made for long, not when she sees your money doubled, maybe even tripled. I'll make one little run over the line, and you'll be all set."

Barney said nobody was getting over the line, you couldn't drive up there the snow was too deep.

Hal told him that was just a matter of good driving and a little shoveling.

"The wedding can't be postponed. Hortense wouldn't stand for that."

"Barney," Hal said, "sit down. I want to talk to you." Barney sat on the bed. "Are you sure you want to marry Hortense?"

"I guess so. We've been engaged for a year."

"How are you going to support her?"

"Hortense wants to keep her job at Sullivan's Cafe, and I've got a new job, besides working for old Hayden at the store. I'm callboy for the conductors."

"Callboy is a rotten job. You've got to go around to the whorehouses and find the bastards, and then make sure they get up after you call them. If they miss the run they blame you. And old Hayden is the meanest man in Minot —he'll work you till you drop, and never give you a raise."

"He's not so bad, Hal. And Hortense says this is just a start, I'll get something better pretty soon. We'll save our money and if something doesn't turn up in Minot we'll go to Spokane."

"There's nothing in Spokane. I just talked to a fellow from there. He came here to look for work."

"We can try, Hal. We've got to try."

"You know what Hortense is? She's your old age trying to catch you before you've had your youth. You ought to have some fun first, kid."

"She isn't even as old as I am, Hal. She's only nineteen."

"That's not what I meant. What time is it? Is the bank open?"

"It's noon."

"Then you can go down and get your money out, and Hortense won't even find out, because I'll be back before Sunday."

"I already took it out for the wedding. And you're not getting it."

Hal pulled on his undershirt and continued the argument. "There is something you ought to know about women. If you give in to Hortense now, she'll have the upper hand all your life. You won't be able to spit without her permission, Barney. Who saved this money, anyway?"

"Well, *I* did, but it's for both of us."

"You save it, it's yours. You can do what you want with it."

"I want to get married with it."

"Look, Barney. How long did you have to work for old Hayden to save twenty-four dollars?"

Barney didn't say.

"You can double it overnight, and no sweat from you at all, I do the work."

A short time later Hal came down to the street, with Barney's twenty-four dollars in the inside pocket of his sheepskin jacket. George went over to his room at the Park Hotel to get his own jacket and a cap with a fur-lined flap that covered his ears and the back of his neck. Hal poured hot water into the radiator of his Buick and by the time George returned he had the engine going. They saw Squeaky Simpson coming along picking his teeth and looking for ways to make some change out of his position as a policeman.

"Where are you two going?" Squeaky demanded, his big chest pushed out in front of his chin, but not in front of his big stomach.

"Around the block," Hal told him. "Got to warm up the engine."

Hal took the shortest way out of town to the road north, and it looked as if the going would be tough, with the snow two feet deep on the level. As they got farther along, there were fewer and fewer tracks, each farmer branching off at his own place, and nobody going anywhere just for pleasure, the way they did in summer. George glanced back at the two shovels on the floor. "I'm not sure I'm going to enjoy the trip," he admitted. "Maybe we ought to think better of it."

"Who started this, George? You got me out of bed to save Minot, and by God we're going to save it. Do you have anything left in that flask of yours?"

George took out the flask and studied it. "I have a feeling we should save this for a real emergency."

Hal said the sky was clear as a bell all the way to the North Pole, and they both took a short swallow.

"You know what that bastard Squeaky wanted me to do when I was a kid? He said I'll watch and you go around the back of Herman's men's store and break in and steal all you can and I'll split with you."

"I have seen him roll more than one unfortunate drunk before he carted him off to the hoosegow. Perhaps he had an unpleasant mother."

Beyond Stanfield the road was not plowed, but the snow crust was hard enough so they could ride on top of the drifts. The going wasn't easy, but it was possible. When they got to Portal they would see Boots Cunningham in the customs house, and Boots might have a little something to renew George's flask.

2

Boots Cunningham was sitting in the customs house at Portal, thinking. He had a view of the prairie through the east window, tufts of taffy-colored grass pricking up through the snow. It was a long, long view, across miles of nothing, and he was damned sick of it. He was sick of this little room, of the file cabinets of papers and letters, of the government pencil in his hand. And most of all he was damned sick of Prohibition. The whole thing was a big crazy mistake, a hilarious joke, a source of trouble and tragedy in which he sometimes was the hammer that came down on the skull. Why should anybody work for a government that made lunacy law?

He went over to the stove and took the boiling coffeepot off, poured himself a cup of thick juice and went outside. As he looked down the Soo Line track, which ran close to the customs house, another uneasiness filled his mind. Boots was pretty sure who was working the racket. Pretty sure. But no solid evidence. He wasn't sure he wanted the solid evidence. What was the harm? In fact, this morning he couldn't say he agreed with the United States in any area where he was supposed not only to agree but to act. To hell with the government.

He threw the terrible coffee on the ground and went inside. He had just sat down again when the door flew open and Hal Brady came in with George Finley.

"I've been expecting you," Boots said. "I hear Minot is dry."

"It is. That's why we came up to the oasis for a drink."

"Come on, Hal. You came up for a load. And you'll never make it through the drifts."

"We made it very well coming up."

"Sit down, thaw out." The phone rang and Boots growled into it. When he hung up he swore. "Mrs. O'Connor. Yesterday she begged me to come out and confiscate Will's moonshine equipment so he'd have to go look for a job and buy his kids some shoes. I'm not supposed to do that kind of work, it's for the Prohis, but I drove out there and dumped his rotten old mash over the bank, packrats and gophers and all, and I hauled away the still. Now she calls me and she's sore as hell. 'You had no business taking my copper boiler, Boots Cunningham! I need that boiler to boil dipers in!'" He grinned, and then his face fell into sour lines. "God, I'm sick of this job. You know what's the matter with this country? Virtue. Skinny-eyed, flat-chested virtue. Think what we all would have been saved if Volstead had been an alcoholic. Virtue carried too far."

"How far is 'too far,' Boots?" George asked.

"About three feet from your back door. Keep your virtue chained, like a pet bulldog who might go out and bite somebody. Want more coffee?"

"Not unless you've got something to kill the taste," Hal told him.

Boots took a bottle from his desk drawer and filled their cups. He also replenished George's flask. "I think I'll quit and go into the cattle business. How about joining me?"

"Sounds good. A customs officer and two bootleggers."

"I mean it. I've got to get out of here before something happens to me."

"No rumrunner would damage you, Boots."

"I wasn't thinking of rumrunners. Forget it. I'm off my feed."

Hal finished his coffee. "Maybe we'll see you on the way back, if conditions are favorable."

"You'd better go around us, Hal. Too many funny things going on right now."

They drove off, and George said, "I wonder what he meant by that?"

"I don't know. Something's eating him."

It was dark when they got to Estavan and saw the rosy windows of the George and Crown, Proprietor Ah Sing. They engaged a room—one dollar for two—and settled before the coal fire.

"What would you like for dinner?" Ah Sing inquired. "We have roast beef, roast pork, roast venison. Roast beef, roast pork all gone."

Ah Sing called the order into the kitchen and came back. Hal had the feeling he was estimating him. "Would you mind, sir, coming with me?"

Hal followed him to a back room, a sort of pantry, where a kettle boiled on a little coal stove. "Tea, sir?"

Hal said yes, out of politeness, he didn't care much for tea. They each drank a cup, and the Chinese still did not explain why they were there. "I should tell you there is a Mountie here, a bad one, he chases Americans over the line."

"That so? Not his job, is it?"

"He has a girl in Minot. Her father is a bootlegger."

"I see. Competition."

Ah Sing nodded. Then, for no reason that Hal could detect, he stacked the teacups and the interview was over.

Hal went back to the table.

"What did he want?" George asked, starting his dinner.

"I don't know. I had a cup of tea, and that was that."

"He must have had something in mind."

"Thought better of it. Maybe I didn't hold the cup correctly."

"This venison is very good. Very good indeed. Why don't we just hole up here for the rest of the winter?"

"What would we use for money?"

"We could go to work in the woods."

"I don't think they have any woods. Anyway, I will never be a lumberjack again."

"Why not? A lumberjack is an honorable man."

"A lumberjack is a lousy man. Have you ever fought graybacks in your drawers, your hair, your bedding, your boots? When I was just a kid I worked for a lumber company in northern Minnesota. They paid your way up from St. Paul, on their own railroad, but they didn't pay your way back unless you stayed thirty days. I stood on a stump for two weeks trying to get fired, but they wouldn't do it. The food was salt pork and potatoes. I finally went over the line to Canada, got a train for Bimidgie and then hopped a Great Northern freight. That was a good train—the engineer told the fireman to tell me to come up and ride near the boiler to keep warm."

"I hear these lumber camps aren't lousy any more—they don't let the men bring in their own bedrolls."

"Maybe. But I never want to work in one again."

George leaned back and smiled. "You know why you don't? You like being shot at. You like being chased."

"Sure. And I like Rosie. You can't take a girl to a lumber camp."

"Are you going to marry Rosie?"

Hal was lighting a cigarette. He looked up sharply. "Hell no. I'm not going to marry anybody. What made you ask that question in the middle of the night in Estavan?"

"I don't know. I guess I wanted the answer."

Hal didn't go on with it—you hardened things if you insisted. Sometimes it was better not to know exactly what someone else meant, especially a good friend like George. But he thought about it. He wondered if George felt the way he did about Rosie. The idea disturbed him. Rosie was his girl, and the thought of her with anybody else, in bed with anybody else—

"I'll tell you why I asked, Hal, so you won't be getting the wrong idea. Rosie is the kind of girl who wants to get married, and if you don't see that, some bookkeeper is going to come along and beat you out."

Hal wanted to know if George and Rosie had talked about this.

"Only once. Rosie said to me, 'I don't think Hal and I will ever get married.'"

"She said that? Why the hell did she say that to you?"

"I'm sorry I brought it up. It's none of my business."

"That's okay. What time did he say the liquor store opens?"

During the night Hal woke. He thought he heard footsteps in the hall, light as mice. He got up, opened the door. Ah Sing's face met his own.

"Oh. Beg pardon, sir. I am coming to speak with you."
"Speak away."
"We have a person here who wants to ride with you."
"You mean over the line?"
Ah Sing nodded.
"A Chinaman?"
"Yes."
Hal shook his head. "I'm sorry."
"Five hundred dollars."
"No. Can't do it." Hal closed the door.

In the morning, after hotcakes and mush, they made their way to the liquor store, bought a case of rye for thirty-six dollars, put the bottles in gunnysacks, tied the sacks with cord and stowed them in the Buick. The road ran alongside the Soo Line tracks, and the going was easy at first, but a factor they hadn't reckoned with brought them to a stop before they got three miles from town. With the added weight of the liquor, the back wheels broke through the snow crust, and the Buick sat with its nose toward the sky and its rear end in a drift. They shoveled out of that one, but immediately sank into another.

George looked back. "I think we have company."
"The border hoppers?"
"The same."

They jumped out and shoveled and spun the wheels and pushed. "Maybe they'll get stuck," Hal suggested.

"They don't have a load. They're traveling on the crust, the way we did coming up."

Hal was facing the bare Soo Line track, kept clear of snow. "Get in, George. I'm going up on the track!" He ran the Buick up the short bank, got one front wheel over the rail, then the back one, and they bumped along with one set of wheels inside and the other outside.

"There's probably a law," George warned.

"Are they catching up?"

The answer came in a crackle of shots. George hunched down in the seat and Hal pushed hard on the gas. "I hope to God they didn't hit the whiskey."

"You can tell by the smell in a couple of minutes."

There were no more shots. That was funny. Hal leaned out and looked back. "They're stuck! By God, they're stuck!"

Close to the border they left the tracks, which went by the customs buildings, veered east to cross and then came back to the railroad. They were a few miles out of Stanfield when George looked at his watch. "The train could be along soon, if it's on time. Better be prepared to get off the line."

Hal had an idea. This early train was a passenger that carried some freight and stopped at every crossroads. They could leave the Buick with Fred Larsen, and ride a boxcar into Minot.

"Who's Fred Larsen?" George wanted to know.

"A farmer. A Swede and a Lutheran, but for a bottle of good Canadian he'll be glad to co-operate. The train stops at Larsen's Crossing long enough for us to stow the whiskey over the trucks. When we get into the yard at Minot, we can grab our booze and run."

George was afraid that somehow they and their investment might become separated. Hal said it couldn't happen, it was all very simple.

They drove into the farmyard and found Fred Larsen hitching a team. They shook hands. "We're been through a little skirmish with the Prohis," Hal explained. "Got a bullet through our rear end, but we still have our whiskey. When is the train due?"

"Anytime now."

"The road is pretty bad with a load on. We'd like to leave the car here for a day or two and ride the train into Minot."

A gleam, connected with thirst, shone in Larsen's eye. "What would you do with the whiskey?"

"We thought we'd stow the stuff on the beam, and then get into a boxcar to keep the bull off the scent."

A boy of sixteen or so came out of the house to see what was going on, and Larsen told him to get back inside. "He's had the flu—not quite over it yet, or else he just doesn't want to go to school."

The kid grinned. "I'm all right, Dad. I'm going back tomorrow."

"Better go in anyway—what you don't know your mother can't find out."

The boy looked disappointed, but he obeyed. Larsen went on, "You're lucky. The cop on this run is usually Dick Scott, but they've got him filling in for a fellow on the other train. I heard he was pretty sore about it, but he's always sore."

"We know him," George said.

They gave Larsen a fifth. They could see the train now, lumbering across the snow-covered prairie, breathing steam. It pulled into the crossing and they stowed a gunnysack over the trucks at each end of the last car, then they climbed into a boxcar, the whistle croaked, and they jerked out of Larsen's crossing.

George wrote something in a matchbook.

"What's that?" Hal asked.

"The number of the car where we put the bottles."

"Why? We know where the bottles are."

"Something might happen."

"Nothing's going to happen."

There were boxes of apples from the Okenagan country in the car, and they had a good fresh smell. The end of the car was partitioned off to keep the fruit away from a kerosene heater, and George sat with his back against this partition to get warm. Hal opened a box of apples.

"There's a funny smell in here," George muttered. "Not kerosene. Not apples. Something else."

"Like what?"

"I don't know. Can't you smell it?"

Hal said he couldn't smell much of anything, his nose had been broken so many times in fights.

George sniffed. "It smells like that hotel in Estavan."

Hal thought it was the carbon monoxide from the heater, but George said there was no odor to that.

They were going along at a good clip when suddenly the rhythm changed. The train slowed, stopped, and Hal opened the door and put his head out. The conductor and the brakeman came along the track, talking.

"Hotbox," Hal decided. "Might take a while."

The engine made short gruff noises, like a horse snorting and pawing, and the steam continued to stream out. A brave passenger or two descended and waded through the snow, arctics flapping and buckles clinking. Their noses got red and then white, and soon they hurried back to the porter with his step, and climbed into the warm car.

"There's a girl in a slicker," Hal reported. "Nothing colder than a slicker. She must be from down south." She came along toward the boxcar, her small face bright and interested, devouring everything.

Hal got down. "Hello," he said. "Aren't you cold?"

"No, not really. I'm wearing two sweaters. That sheepskin looks wonderful. I've always wanted one. Girls don't get them, you know. I did have a skunk jacket."

"Did the conductor say how long we'd be here?"

"No, they never tell you. You know how it is when the train is late getting into Minot; you could sit in that damned depot for three hours, and they'd still be telling you it was only twenty minutes late."

"You're from Minot, then?"

"Yes. Where are *you* from?"

"Minot."

"I'm on my way home from school. I got expelled."

"How nice. What for?"

"Smoking. They'll probably take me back if I want to go. I'm not sure I want to. What's your philosophy of life?"

There was a sudden bustling and shouting along the track, the conductor, cried, "All aboard," the porter began handing people up the steps.

"I'd better run. Maybe I'll see you sometime in Minot." The girl gave him a serious, intense look, like a carpenter nailing down a shingle, wham. Then she turned her face to the wind and trotted off.

"What's your name?" Hal called.

"Wanda." She kept on running.

"Last name?"

She was beyond the sound of his voice, and he saw her jump up the steps like a little rabbit and disappear.

Hal climbed back when the conductor had his attention elsewhere.

"Who was the little canary in the yellow overcoat?" George asked.

"Never saw her before, but she's from Minot."

"I can't believe you didn't get her name."

"She said she had a skunk jacket, but she wasn't wearing it. She was thrown out of school for smoking."

"Maybe the school kept the jacket. Very mercenary bastards running these boarding schools."

"Boarding school? She looks too old for that. Maybe nineteen."

"A great age indeed, nineteen."

"She asked me what my philosophy of life was."

George laughed. "She's nineteen."

When the train eased into the yard at Minot, they swung off and headed for the car where the liquor was stowed.

Hal was reaching for one of the gunnysacks when a blue uniform came toward them, bellowing. They ducked around to the other side of the car, waited for him to go away. But he didn't go away. He stood there, his big feet planted, his little eyes watching. There was a bustle of activity around the freight, the whistle blew, and the cop turned and swung on.

"It can't be pulling out!" Hal cried.

The wheels turned, the couplings clanked, and the train jerked through the yard.

"There goes Barney's money," George muttered.

"We're not giving up yet. We can catch it with the eastbound passenger train."

"Where? St. Paul?"

Hal went into the depot and looked at the blackboard. They had an hour and a half to wait, if the train was on time. They spent the time in a small steamy cafe and were ready when the passenger engine roared in.

They swung on, pulled themselves into the blinds, and in a few moments the trucks were hitting the joints in the rails, cadump, cadump, cadump. Hal said if he'd had a little more education he could figure out where and how soon they would catch up with the freight, but George said you couldn't figure that even with an education—a lot of things happened to trains in a North Dakota winter.

It was getting colder and they were hungry. George said maybe it was all for nothing, if they dropped that car off at some little town they could never find it.

"We'll find it."

It was well into the night when they pulled into a small deserted depot, let off a lady with a child and a grip, and almost immediately began to ease out again.

There was a freight waiting on the siding, and George cried, "That's it, Hal, that's our car!"

They scrambled down, stiff with cold, and ran toward the last boxcar. They reached it, carefully pulled out the gunnysacks still bulging and no tinkle of broken glass.

"I'll watch this stuff while you find out when the westbound goes through," George offered.

The stationmaster was ready to lock the depot with its good coal fire.

"Is there a westbound coming through anytime soon?" Hal asked.

"Passenger is due at 4:20 A.M."

"Could you let my friend come in and get warm before you lock up?"

"Sure, why not?" He was a quick, bright-eyed little man and he shook the fire down to a red-hot bed of coals. George came in and Hal went out to guard the gunnysacks, then he decided there wasn't anybody around for miles in the cold prairie night, and came in again.

"Sorry I have to lock up." The stationmaster was apologetic. "I have to get forty winks before the westbound comes in."

They thanked him, and went outside. "Does it strike you we're going through a hell of a lot for Barney's bank account?" Hal asked.

They waited, the stars sharp as ice over their heads, a little wind riffling the tan grass that came out of the snow. At last the stationmaster came back, they got warm again, and then the train whistled, the lights shone on the polished steel track, and they swung aboard.

It was very cold standing in the blinds on the sliding iron plates that hinged over the coupling. If you sat down the cold ran right up your spine.

Hal never had a watch, but George looked at his from time to time, and when the first gray light showed the fences and ditches, he announced what the Pullman passengers were doing. "The waiter in his starched white coat with only one gravy spot is now going through, beating his gong and announcing, 'First call for breakfast.' They turn over, they raise the dark green shades and look out but they can't see a damned thing. They sit up and find their underpants and socks in the green cord hammock."

"How do you know so much about life on a Pullman?"

"I once rode a Pullman, when I had funds. I almost think I prefer it to our present accommodations. Although if you're tall you may bump your head when you sit up in an upper berth. Anyway, they fight their way into their trousers, take their razors and sway back to the washroom, where they run nice hot water into a shiny metal basin, dry their faces on clean white towels with a red stripe and maybe they swipe a towel or two. They go into the tight little toilet and hang onto a bar while they pee and the train swings around a curve. Ever hear the song about that? Undoubtedly composed by one of the great railroad magnates:

> "'We encourage constipation
> While the train is in the station
> I love you.'"

"Hurry up and get them to the dining car," Hal pleaded. "I want to hear what the bastards are having for breakfast."

"Anything their little hearts desire. Ham and eggs. Hot cream of wheat with real cream. Beautiful hot black coffee in a silver pitcher, with more cream in another silver pitcher. Oregon plums. California grapefruit. A rose in a silver vase. Pancakes and rivers of syrup. Mounds of butter in ice."

"Never mind the ice. I don't think I was ever so cold in my life."

The sun now made the prairie blinding white, but there was no warmth in it. They stamped their feet and rubbed their hands, and Hal began to feel numb. He looked at George. "Wake up, you idiot, you're falling asleep."

At the next stop George climbed down to walk the platform and get his blood moving. He came back quickly. "They're going to add a couple of boxcars."

A car knocker came along, and he seemed friendly, so Hal asked him if the cars would be empty.

"Sure. You rather ride inside?"

"Wouldn't you?"

"Watch out for the bull on this train. Son-of-a-bitch."

They thanked him and scrambled down on the far side, taking their sacks. When the switch engine brought up the empty cars they lifted their sacks into the first one and climbed in after them. The car already had five occupants, a woman and two children huddled in newspapers at the end, and a couple of young fellows from Georgia, thinly dressed.

George and Hal were examined critically by five pairs of eyes, then the boys became friendly. The one named Chuck did most of the talking, his friend Joe listened and smiled. They had a worn old satchel that contained everything they owned, and they were going to look for work in Minot. Hal told them there was no work in Minot, in fact he didn't know where there was any work.

"How about Spokane?" Chuck asked.

George shook his head. "How is it down south?"

"Bad. Nobody's working. There's four kids younger than me, so I thought I should get out and be on my own. Joe's got three sisters."

The woman didn't say a word, and Hal thought maybe he and George were a little frightening, with a good growth of beard and probably a good smell of whiskey about them.

"She's going to the coast," Chuck whispered. "No money. Kids haven't eaten anything since we got on yesterday afternoon."

Hal wanted to get off and get some sandwiches, but George said he'd be left behind, the train was ready to pull out.

"I can make it." Hal dropped off into the yard, picked his way across the tracks, and spotted the Owl Cafe. The inside of the Owl smelled like its name, but it was warm, and the Chinaman got the idea instantly that speed was important. He dropped a loaf of bread, a slab of butter, and some hot roast pork into a paper bag, and said fifty cents. Hal gave it to him and ran back. The train was already moving, but with the help of George and the two boys and the loss of a little skin, he pulled himself in.

The smell of the warm roast pork was too much for the woman. She smiled, and helped butter the bread after George cut it in ragged chunks with his knife.

"I didn't have time to get coffee," Hal explained. "Anybody care for a swallow of Canadian whiskey?"

The boys accepted at once, but the woman shook her head. The children, not wonderfully full but partly satisfied, fell asleep.

Hal and George crawled into a corner of the car, the gunnysacks between them, and slept. Hal was wakened by a heavy voice growling, "Open it up. Let's see what you've been stealing." A railroad bull in a blue uniform stood over the boys from Georgia poking their satchel with his foot.

"We ain't been stealin' nothin'," Chuck told him.

"Open it up. Dump out your truck."

They emptied the satchel on the floor of the car. The bull spotted a pair of new shoes. "Where'd you get a good pair of shoes like that? Stole 'em, didn't you?"

"No, I didn't," Joe cried. "My dad and my uncle went together and give me five dollars to get a pair of good shoes, in case I got work."

The officer took off his right shoe, slid his foot into the new one, seemed to like the fit. He picked up the pair, threw down a dollar bill, and started for the door. The train was slowing down.

"Mister, you can't—I need them shoes!"

George sat up. "Dick Scott, as I live and breathe."

The bull turned on him. Hal stood up, his fists ready. "Just give the boy his shoes, and we'll call it square."

Scott glared, but he dropped the shoes and swung off as the train slowed. Hal looked out and saw they were in the yard at Minot.

"We'll have one hell of a time getting past him with our stuff now," Hal warned.

"You shouldn't of made him mad," Joe said. "He could have you in jail."

"We've got more friends in Minot than Dick Scott has in the whole country," George told him. "And you don't need to be afraid of him, this is the end of his run for tonight. You just stay on here."

Hal and George gave the woman what little money they had left, and swung off the car with their sacks.

"Funny he gave up without pulling his gun," Hal reflected.

"His position wasn't very good—two witnesses saw him try to steal a pair of shoes."

"I'd have enjoyed a good fight."

"One is bound to come along. In fact, it might be here right now."

A large blue figure loomed in front of them. They ran, Dick Scott after them, and got out of the yard to the street. The first door was Wong's Hand Laundry, and they ducked in.

Wong had his iron on a shirt. His hand stopped. "Something?" he inquired.

"Whiskey," Hal told him. "Where can we hide it?"

He led them into the steamy back room, pointed to a mound of sheets. They buried the sacks, and squeezed into a closet as the front door banged open.

"Where are they?" Scott bellowed.

"Nobody here, mister officer," Wong told him.

"The hell there ain't. I saw them come in here, two bums with sacks over their shoulders." He came into the back room and began kicking the mound of sheets. He found the whiskey. "So this is what they had. No wonder they ran. Come on out, I know you're here."

"No, they go out back door," Wong insisted.

"We'll just confiscate this stuff and report you to the Prohis for protecting bootleggers." He picked up one sack and was trying to manage the other when Hal and George came at him from the closet, grabbed him by the legs and threw him.

"You hold him down and I'll take off his shoes," George ordered.

They left him flailing around in the dirty sheets, and followed Wong out the back door.

"Come with me!" Wong ran down the alley, his white shirt flying.

They caught up with him in the next block as he burst in at the back door of the Red Pagoda. Another Chinaman was cooking something in a big iron skillet.

"My cousin Sidney," Wong bowed.

"What's wrong?" Sidney inquired.

"They have whiskey. You need some?"

Sidney, trying to conceal his eagerness, moved with caution. "Who made this?"

"It's good Canadian, the genuine article," George told him.

Sidney examined the seals. "How much?"

"A hundred and fifty."

"One hundred."

"You're dreaming," Hal told him. "Everybody in Minot

has their tongue hanging out for stuff like this. One hundred fifty and not a cent less."

"Okay." Sidney laid the bills in Hal's palm.

"What about me?" Wong demanded. "I bring him here."

Sidney reopened his wallet, took out a ten, looked at it, put it back and took out a five.

"Give him the ten," George persuaded.

"Yes. I lose a customer over this. Mr. Scott from railroad. Maybe he comes back to beat me up."

Sidney gave him the ten, and Wong hurried off.

"Besides that, I think he burned up a shirt," Hal remarked, as he and George went out the front door to Central Avenue.

They went into Sullivan's and took a table at the back, in case Scott should come along and look in the window.

They had just sat down when the kitchen door swung open and Hortense came flying through with a big tray of cups. When she saw Hal her small sharp eyes blazed. He thought he was going to get the cups right in the chest.

"Where's Barney's twenty-four dollars?" she demanded.

"Right here." Hal patted his pants pocket. "And twenty-four more to go with it, Hortense."

"I don't believe it. Let's see it."

Hal showed her.

"Give it to me, now."

"I don't give Barney's money to anybody but Barney."

"Give it to me. You won't have it two hours."

"Come on, Hortense. We're two hungry frozen men, and we want some steaks. How about it?"

"Not until you turn over Barney's money."

Sullivan strolled over. "Hello, Hal. Hello, Finley. How's it going?"

Hortense took their orders and stamped back to the kitchen. Sullivan grinned. "She's good help, but she's a bulldog for getting her own way. God help your poor brother."

"Poor old Barney," Hal agreed. "I wish there was a way to change his mind."

"He wouldn't dare, now."

"Maybe Hortense is not a mistake, from Barney's point of view," George suggested. "She puts a high value on Barney."

"She won't let him pee in private."

In a few minutes Hortense brought their steaks, hot, brown and tough, slammed down bottles of ketchup, Worcestershire, A-1 and mustard. "If you lose that money, Hal, I'll never speak to you again."

"That will be a terrible punishment, dear. When is the wedding?"

"Sunday. You knew that. Barney said he told you."

"I was just hoping you'd put it off awhile, till he got a better job."

"We're not putting it off, we can get along fine on what we both bring in." She looked thoughtful, and her voice had a more gentle tone. "Why don't you get married, Hal? You need somebody to steady you."

"Don't try to run the whole family, Hortense."

She went off, and George said, "You hurt her feelings."

"I'm not sure she has feelings. She reminds me of a file on a saw blade."

In a few minutes Barney came in. Hortense must have phoned him. "Did you get it?"

"We got it." Hal took the money, counted forty-eight dollars into Barney's hand.

"Thanks, Hal. Thanks a lot."

Hortense was right there. "You'd better let me have it before he gets it away from you again."

"He doubled our money, Hortense. You ought to thank him."

"Let me bank it, Barney."

He gave it to her, a little reluctantly, and then he sat down and had some beef stew.

High Ass Swede came in, looking very happy for a Swede. "You know what happened? That son of a bitch Dick Scott met up with a couple of bad characters and they took his shoes away from him. He had to walk home in his socks. He must of damned near froze to death."

"I told you it was too cold for him to go barefoot, Hal," George said.

"You two was the ones done it? Geez, he'll kill you. He'll really kill you."

"He'll have to catch us first." George folded his share of the whiskey money into his pocket. "I don't know why, but I'm tired. I think I might even take a nap."

Hal went back to his room and found a note from Rosie: "Where did you go? Why didn't you leave a message?"

He grinned, and fell into bed.

3

Hal woke to find Rosie sitting on the bed, looking at him. He pulled her down, and her warm arms went round his neck.

"You look awful. Where were you?"

"George and I went up to Estavan. We got a case and sold it to the Red Pagoda."

"You didn't take Dick Scott's shoes, did you? Swede said you did, but I told him you had better sense than to mix with a railroad bull."

"We didn't take his shoes. You should know Swede gets things wrong most of the time."

She sat up. "I think you did. I can tell when you're lying, you do it so well. You do it better than ordinary talking."

He pulled her down again, kissed her neck. "What have you been up to, Rosie?"

"Nothing. I might have to go up to Stanfield."

"Something wrong at your sister's?"

"You know Mary's girls have been saving for a pony."

"I know you've been saving for a pony for Mary's girls."

"It isn't just money I sent them. They earned some of it themselves, washing dishes and milking."

"Milking? Those little kids?"

"Freda is eleven. She's a good little worker, and her dad pays her well. Anyway, they finally saved up twenty-five dollars, and they could buy a nice pony for that from a neighbor, but they can't get their money out of the bank."

"Why not?"

"That little weasel says they can't take it out till they've had it in there a year. He just made that up to keep their money, the poor little girls."

"Who is the weasel?"

"The president of the bank, of course. J. Robert Dahl, and I always thought he was a nice fellow. He wanted me to marry him when I was in high school."

"Why didn't you?"

"His feet were too small."

Hal stuck one foot out from under the covers. "How are mine for size?"

Her shrewd gray eyes narrowed. "Are you asking me to marry you, Hal?"

He held her tight. "Rose, you know you don't want to marry a bootlegger."

"I'm living with one. You've got my morals so scrambled up, Hal Brady, that I don't know what's right and what's wrong."

He kissed her on the ear.

"Stop, I've got to be at work in twenty minutes." Rosie worked at the Prairie Dog, a high-class speakeasy.

He tweaked the nipples on her small round breasts. Rosie said, "Damn you," but she liked it.

She still had her head on his chest when he said, "Do you know a girl named Wanda?"

She sat up. "Wanda who?"

"I don't know her last name."

"I'm sure you'll find out." Rosie jumped out of bed, ran hot water into the basin.

"I didn't mean to make you mad."

She didn't say anything. She scrubbed her face hard, with soap, got into the blue wool dress she wore to work.

"I'll walk you to work. George and I had to leave the car at Stanfield."

"Never mind." She yanked on her coat and slammed out the door. He could hear her indignant high heels clumping down the stairs. Women were funny about when you brought up something. Hal went back to sleep, his money under his pillow and the door locked.

When he woke again it was nearly midnight, time to see what was going on in Minot. He shaved and put on a clean shirt and his sheepskin, and went out into the crackling cold night. There were spears of light going up from every streetlight, something to do with the frost crystals in the air, and it was beautiful. You couldn't take a deep breath or you'd freeze your lungs, but it was beautiful. He hurried over the icy walks to the Park Hotel, and went downstairs where they had dancing. The drinks tonight were some bad beer a fellow had stolen and stored in a silo, where it froze. Everybody had the scours, but they kept on drinking it because there wasn't anything else right now.

It was nice and warm. They had steam heat in the hotel, and the place was as full as it could get and still leave a six-foot space for dancing. He squeezed down at a table with Lucy Pepetino and a couple of fellows from the flour mill lucky enough to have jobs. Lucy was a good dancer, and he spun her around the floor a couple of times.

"How's Rosie?" she asked.

"Fine."

"I hear Dick Scott lost his shoes." She gave him a nice smile from her heavy brown eyes. "I guess you don't know anything about that, do you, Hal?"

"Not a thing. Hadn't heard it."

"You'd better look out. My dad says he's dynamite."

As they wormed their way back to the table, a gust of cold air came down the stairs from the open door, and another couple came in.

"She's a new one," Lucy said. "I never saw her before."

Hal had seen her. Wanda was wearing a muskrat coat and a pink silk scarf and was looking as if this was what she did every night. The boy with her looked scared. She saw Hal and waved.

"She knows you." Lucy was surprised. "Who is she?"

"Her name is Wanda, and she owns a yellow slicker. That's all I know."

Hal took Lucy to her table, turned around to find Wanda and her friend standing behind him.

"There isn't a table in the place," she told him. "We'll sit with you."

"Those chairs belong to my friends." Lucy's voice was sharp. "They're dancing."

"We'll leave when they come back."

Her friend protested. "You can't take somebody else's table, Wanda."

"I'll be dancing, and you look around for a place, Woodrow." Wanda took Hal by the hand and led him to the dance floor.

She was a terrible dancer, and he was glad the floor was so crowded nobody could see how they were doing.

"I'm not good, but I can learn." She smiled up at him.

"You've got the nerve of Willy Riley and the three

McGees. What's your last name? Does your mother know where you are?"

"No. But I don't worry about her. Do you come here all the time?"

"Now and then. You didn't say what your name is."

"What's yours?"

"I'll take you back to your boyfriend now, and he'd better get you out of here."

"Why?"

"This is no place for you. You're too young."

Another burst of cold air came down the stairs. Hal had his back to the entrance and didn't see who came in, but he had a feeling something was wrong. He let go of Wanda and turned, in time to catch the full blow on his nose. He lost his balance and went down among the dancers. When he got to his feet, Wanda was leaving very fast in the custody of a large man in a dark-blue overcoat.

A couple of friends sat Hal on a chair. "He really landed that one, Hal."

"Who was he?"

"Didn't you see him? Dick Scott. That's his daughter. You didn't bring her here, did you, Hal?"

"No, she came with some young fellow. She just danced with me while he looked for a table. I don't know her at all."

"But you know Dick Scott, from what I hear. Somebody took his shoes and he had to walk home in his socks. It made him kind of sore."

Hal didn't feel equal to explaining anything right then. Lucy came over and said it served him right, dancing with a kid like that, old Scott was a rat, but he had a right to protect his girl from a wild guy like Hal.

"I'm not a wild guy," Hal protested. "I told the kid to go home, she had no business here."

Lucy and some other girl wiped up the blood on his shirt and his face with a towel from the washroom. It was a good wool shirt and he hated to see it destroyed. Maybe Rosie could clean it.

He began to feel a little better and was thinking of moving on to the Prairie Dog, when a girl from one of the Houses on Third Avenue came down with more cold air, and looked the place over as if she wanted to find somebody. When she saw Hal, she came right over.

"I've got to talk to you, Mr. Brady. Can you come outside?"

"What for? It's damned cold out there."

"Come on, you won't be sorry."

He picked up his jacket and followed her up the stairs. "Let's go into the hotel lobby where it's warm."

"No, somebody might see us. This has got to be quiet. Listen, there's a fellow from Minneapolis with a carful of alcohol—it's parked out in front of the House, and he's inside drunk."

"Nobody's been getting through. You sure it's alcohol?"

"Yes, I'm sure. He's been hiding out, waiting for the price to go up."

"Keys in the car?"

"No."

"By the way, do I know you?"

"I'm Violet—from Mae Munroe's place."

He remembered. "I didn't know you, Violet, without your dog." She always carried a toy bulldog named Shamrock. Shamrock had a mean beady eye and a constant dirty snuffle. Violet loved him above everything else in the world.

"Shamrock has a cold, so I left him with one of the girls."

"How much do you want out of this?"

"Half."

"Half? That's pretty steep, Violet."

"If it's too much, I'll be glad to have whatever you think is right."

Hal patted her arm. "It's not too much. I always say it's too much, that's a rule in this business. I'll see what I can do." He let her walk on ahead, and followed at a distance. The car was there all right, and loaded. There was nobody in sight, and it wasn't the kind of night when people hung around to watch what other people might be doing.

He got into the Ford, released the brake, put it in gear and then got out and pushed. If he could get it down the hill and into Shorty Bauer's driveway, he could unload it there into another vehicle, and drive it away. He didn't want to get caught with this particular car.

The Ford was hard to push, everything on it was stiff. Finally it began to move, and he jumped in and steered it downhill, around the curve and into the driveway. The house was dark, and that was both good and bad. If the door was locked he couldn't use the phone, but he would avoid splitting with Shorty, who was a hog in a deal. Hal rang the bell, waited. No sounds from inside, so he tried the door. It opened into Shorty's front hall, dark and smelling of home brew and sauerkraut. The phone was on the wall beside the coat rack, and he was waiting for the taxi to answer when Shorty came stumbling down the stairs in the dark.

"Who's there? What the hell do you want?" Shorty

pulled a string, and a bulb glared. "Hal, what are you doin' in my house, on my phone?"

"Sorry, Shorty, I thought you were out someplace, and I had to use your phone to call a taxi."

"What do you want a taxi for?" Shorty was wearing a gray flannel nightshirt and a mackinaw. He needed a shave.

"I might as well tell you, because you'll find out anyway. I've got a load in a car outside in your driveway, and I've got to put it in a safe location for the night."

Shorty said this was not a safe location, they were watching him all the time, they thought he was a big operator and he wished it was true. "I'm too dumb to be a success in this business. I stick to plumbing, I know plumbing. So get your load out of my driveway and off my place, Brady."

The taxi driver came on and said he'd be right up. It took him a while, and Shorty got very jumpy, peeking out his hall window every two minutes to see if the Feds were coming. Hal gave him five dollars for his nerves, and then the taxi arrived. Hal and the driver began to unload the whiskey while Shorty stood on the front porch wringing his hands and urging them to hurry.

"Shut up and carry a few cases," Hal ordered.

Shorty went inside and came out again in a pair of arctics, the buckles clanking and rattling, and his teeth chattering.

When they got the stuff transferred to the taxi, Hal and the driver got in.

"Hey, you, wait a minute!" Shorty cried. "What about this car?"

"I've got to leave it here for a short time," Hal told him.

"As soon as I've delivered the stuff I'll be back and pick up the Ford and you'll be all clear."

"You can't leave me with a bootlegger's car in my driveway! They'll arrest me, Hal. I'll go to jail!"

Hal gave him another five dollars for his nerves, and they drove over to the Prairie Dog.

The Prairie Dog served the best liquor available at any given time, and Homer would pay a fair price for the alcohol. When Hal got there nearly everybody had left, but Rosie was serving a final round to three rails at a table at the far end of the room.

"Pretty quiet," he said to Homer. "Business falling off?"

"We had quite a run on the toilets, Hal, due to that damned frosted beer. I think they couldn't wait, so they went home to use their own. What's with you?"

"I know where there's a load of prime alocohol out of Minneapolis."

"Is it for sale?"

"I kind of promised Charlie Van—"

"Come on, Hal, Charlie never pays a decent price. I'll give you twelve dollars a gallon."

"Sold."

Rosie came over. "I'm about ready to go home, Hal. You can take me."

"I thought maybe you'd still be sore."

"You know I don't stay mad."

"I know. That's one of the many good things about you, honey." Hal unloaded the alcohol and then he took Rosie home in the taxi.

"I've got a little job to do, and then I'll be back," he told her.

"Is it something dangerous?"

"No, all I have to do is move a car."

She gave him a suspicious look, went on in.

Hal told the driver to drop him off at Shorty's. Shorty wasn't bad at starting a car, especially when he wanted to get rid of it. They got the Ford going, with a few wiring adjustments and a kettle of hot water, and Hal chugged off, the taxi following. He left the car about a mile out of town, on the highway east. The fellow from Minneapolis would be able to locate it sooner or later.

On the way back, Hal sniffed the early morning air, noted a certain softening, a certain dampness, almost like the smell of spring, and he thought there might be a Chinook coming. If he was right, and he generally was about weather, he might be able to get through to Wisconsin.

Rosie was in bed in her pink crepe-de-chine nightgown with her eyes shut.

Hal said, "I found out who she is."

The eyes flew open. "Who *who* is?"

"Wanda. She's Dick Scott's daughter."

"So?"

"He didn't like it when I danced with her in the Park."

"I don't like it either. What are you up to with this girl, Hal?"

"Nothing. She's just a kid. Got thrown out of her school back East for smoking."

"And how did this innocent child happen to be in a place where she would be dancing with a bootlegger?"

"She and a young fellow came in. They couldn't find a table so they latched onto Lucy Pepetino. Then she wanted to dance with me—"

"Then?"

"Scott came looking for her, and he didn't care much

for me even before that because of the shoes, so he hit me."

"Good. I hope it hurt. Now let me get my sleep. I have the day shift tomorrow at The Dog."

It took him some time to pull off his socks and get into his flannel pajamas. He hated flannel pajamas, they were too hot, but Rosie insisted on them. No matter how easy a person's viewpoint was in most ways, they always had some ironclad rules they wanted you to follow.

He thought about the people he knew, and how their minds worked. A dog had sound reasons for everything he did. A horse the same. But people— / He thought about his mother, and her fear that God would punish Hal for his wicked life, but at the same time she was willing, before she died, to take money that came from this life. She didn't seem to understand that with times like they were, a fellow had to do whatever he could, whatever the country offered him, to keep eating. He had tried riding the boxcars all over the country, looking for work, cooking under bridges in tin cans, picking up quarters for odd jobs and feeling sorry for the men who couldn't find a quarter. One summer he and Al McDougal had painted half the Elks' flagpoles in the Northwest, they got twenty to thirty dollars a pole, and it was a good thing while it lasted. He remembered the day they put aluminum paint on the courthouse flagpole in Coos Bay, Oregon. There was a nice breeze blowing, and when they got through, half the cars in town had aluminum polka dots.

He looked down at Rosie, already asleep. She shouldn't be working in the Prairie Dog. Rosie wasn't meant to be a bar girl, but that was all she could get to do right now and she was a logical person—about everything but flannel pajamas.

He stopped thinking about Rosie. Boots Cunningham, too, was a logical person. He didn't lose sleep over trivialities like rum-running, smuggling, crazy Prohis and crazier bootleggers. It must be something else. Something serious. What was going on up there at the border?

In the morning when he came down, Mrs. Murphy came out of the cigar store and said some girl had called him at half-past nine. "I knew you weren't awake yet, so I told her to call back sometime. Rosie was burned up about it."

"How did Rosie happen to know about it?"

"I told her. She came down just as I hung up the phone, and I told her." Mrs. Murphy enjoyed trouble, and made quite a lot of it. She was a sharp-nosed, tight-muscled woman, she made you think of a car wired for a bomb. Everybody liked Toni. When he neglected to give you heat in the dead of winter, it didn't seem as cold in your room as when Ada refused to open up the furnace.

"Who was the girl?" Hal asked, knowing quite well.

"Search me. She gave a number, but I don't know where I put it."

"Never mind. I don't want to talk to her anyway."

"How do you know, if you don't know who she is?"

Hal stepped out into the sunny morning, and the warm air stopped him on the doorstep. It was a Chinook. He took off his sheepskin and walked along in his shirt. Everybody was out in their shirtsleeves, celebrating, except Squeaky Simpson, the cop, who had no blood anyway. Squeaky was hanging around in front of Hennessy's restaurant with a toothpick in his teeth. He did that so everybody would think he had just eaten and it was safe to say, "Can I buy you a cup of coffee, Squeaky?" Then Squeaky would say, "Sure," and come inside and eat steak and eggs and hotcakes and a side of prunes.

Inside, George Finley was at the counter, having sourdoughs and sorghum. "Hal, we've got to depart immediately for a run to Stevens Bend. Olsen has everything set, and every speakeasy in town is ready to pay any price for good uncut alcohol. Our share will be generous. We can become temporarily solvent."

That reminded Hal he hadn't paid Violet on the Hill for her tip on the Minneapolis load. He'd better do that right away.

"Olsen wants us to use his cars, not take the time to go after yours. He thinks the warm spell could end suddenly. Of course he's right."

"I'd rather drive the Buick."

"I know, but we can't waste the time, Hal."

Before Hal's toast was ready, Violet came in. "I want my share," she said. "I want my money right away."

"You're going to have it right away." Hal took out his money clip. "Did our friend sober up yet?"

"Yes, and he's wild. He found his car, but his boots and gun were gone. Did you have anything to do with that, Mr. Brady?"

"I didn't even see any boots or gun. They must have been taken while his car was out in front of the house."

She looked at him a minute. "I believe you. But you'd better stay out of sight for a few days. He might think you had the boots and guns, and he's more for hunting than he is for bootlegging."

They were finishing breakfast when Barney walked in, his cheeks pink from fresh air, his dark curly brown hair shining.

"You're coming to the wedding, aren't you, Hal? We want you and Rosie to be there Sunday."

Hal thought what a shame to turn this good human specimen over to Hortense and her long nose. "Barney, call your boss and say you're laying off for a couple of days. We're going to Stevens Bend and we need you to drive. With the three of us, we can travel day and night. You can make enough out of the trip to pay your rent for six months."

"I can't lay off. Old Hayden would fire me."

"You can be sick. He's got pneumonia, hasn't he, George?"

"Looks like it to me. You look very bad, Barney."

"She has the wedding planned for Sunday, church and all."

"We'll be back Saturday morning."

"It's dangerous, you could get shot."

"There's no danger in it, Barney. Clear sailing to Stevens Bend, we're met by the sheriff, who is also the alcohol merchant, we pick up our load, have a good sleep and start out early the next morning for home."

Barney was weakening, Hal could see it. "I'll take you over to your room and you can get some heavy socks and everything warm you own, in case it turns cold again."

On the way, they stopped at the Prairie Dog to say goodbye to Rosie. She was slicing liverwurst and cheese for the free lunch, and she looked frightened when he told her about the trip.

"I wish you wouldn't go, Hal."

"I've done it before, Rosie. There's nothing to it. Would I take Barney if it was dangerous?"

"You're taking your brother?"

"Sure—Barney, you'd better phone old Hayden at the grocery and whoever you report to at the G.N. yard."

"I have to say goodbye to Hortense."

"She'll talk you out of it. Phone Sullivan's and leave a message."

"I don't know what to say."

Rosie told him. "Just say your wonderful brother Hal has talked you into risking your life for a few lousy dollars. He thinks it's fun—but it won't be fun for you, Barney. You'll be scared stiff."

"I guess I could take a chance," Barney muttered. "I ought to do one crazy thing before I get married."

"Goodbye, Rosie." Hal patted her gently on the head—he never patted her rear in public. "We'll be back in a couple of days, and don't worry."

"I'm not worrying. I'll have a good time while you're gone."

"Don't let her, Homer. Keep an eye on her."

Rosie watched him go, and returned to the job of cutting cheese. These damned bootleg runs, he could get shot—

Homer saw that she was crying. "He'll come through all right, Rosie. He always does. You want the day off to go up and see your sister in Stanfield?"

She was grateful. That would take her mind off Hal, and she could maybe think of a way to get the girls' money out of J. Robert Dahl's bank. "Know what I think? That bank is going to fail. He's hanging on to every dime he can."

Homer agreed. Most banks were failing, so why not the bank at Stanfield? "It's pretty cheap, when you have to rob three little girls."

Rosie took the bus. On the way, looking out the steamed window at the beige fields of stubble and snow, she thought about Hal. He was awful, he was always doing something crazy, illegal, dangerous. But there was nobody like him, there was nobody else who could make her elbows melt when she saw him come into a room. She ought not to be living with him, that was wrong, it wasn't what she had been brought up to at all. A girl should be careful. Even Hortense, homely and harsh as she was, had captured a good, kind, faithful person to be her husband. But Barney wasn't Hal. There was nothing unexpected about Barney, that was the whole thing. You couldn't spend your life with a foregone conclusion.

Maybe I should never had come down to Minot to work. If I'd stayed up in Stanfield I wouldn't have met Hal Brady. I could give him up. He thinks he can do what he wants and I'll accept it. Like Wanda Scott. Her neck got hot when she thought about the way he had brought up Wanda. That was outrageous.

They passed a couple of potholes where the snow had dark patterns, melting into the ice, and a hawk circled, looking for mice or gophers. That was another thing about Hal—he noticed every living creature that moved in the landscape, he could tell you all about its habits, its home, its disposition. That was nice.

The bus driver talked with the woman in the front seat across from him—long, slow, easy talk, about the weather and the winter-wheat crop, and the low prices, and what good did it do a farmer to grow anything if he couldn't get a decent price, and the state of North Dakota was going to own all the farms if things went on this way, and did you know the priest and Mrs. Jordan split up, he was living there but he moved his socks, and Art Olsen had sold a sheep for the price of a haircut, and the bank in Stanfield seemed to be holding out. Bob Dahl was a pretty shrewd fellow, but you never could tell.

There were only a handful of people on the bus, and the journey was quiet, almost sleepy. Rosie looked out the window and felt herself detached, flying along in the landscape without ties, without obligations or demands on herself from the people around her. It was good to be by yourself, to think your own thoughts, to see everything you know from a little distance. Not as if you were giving it all up—not that certainly—but to see it as if you could give it all up.

Mary, fresh and pretty in her starched gingham house dress, listened to Rosie's plan to take the girls out of school at recess in order to go to the bank. "I don't think Harry would want them to miss school," she objected.

"We've got to get there before the bank closes or nothing will work."

"What do you mean, nothing will work? What are you going to do, Rosie?"

"I'm not going to do anything. Just be with them, and see that they get a fair deal."

"You know the bank won't let them have their money."

"We'll see. You'll have to write a note to allow them to leave school for a half hour."

"I don't think I should—Harry—"

"Oh, damn Harry. They want their money and we're going to get it."

Mary sighed, wrote the note. "If you'd just married Bob Dahl this would never have happened. He'd have had to let them take out their money."

"Would you want me to be a living sacrifice for twenty-five dollars?" Rosie took the note and the bankbook and walked over to the grade school.

The girls were delighted to be taken out, especially by their Aunt Rose. They listened attentively to her instructions, and Freda, the eldest and most confident, took the bankbook. The bank was within twenty minutes of closing and had a rush of customers—five people in line at the teller's window, another looking into his wallet, a woman writing a check at the counter. Mr. Dahl was not in sight, and the teller looked unfriendly.

Rose put Freda in line with Julie on one side and the little one, Gertrude, on the other. The line moved slowly, and Gertrude complained, "I'm tired, Aunt Rose. When will we get our money?"

"Your turn is coming, dear. Just be patient."

Finally Freda reached the window, and scared but determined, slid the open book under the grille. "We want to take our money out."

The teller craned his stringy neck and looked over the counter at the three. "Little girl, we told you—Mr. Dahl himself told you—you cannot withdraw a savings account in less than a year's time."

"We want our money now."

"You cannot withdraw the account until a year has passed."

Gertrude looked at Rosie. "Now, Aunt Rose?"

"Now."

Gertrude let out a howl. Rosie, with the corner of her eye, saw the woman look up, alarmed. The two men going out the door hesitated, came back. Gertrude dropped to the floor, kicking and screaming. "I want my pony! Aunt Rose said we could have a pony. I want my pony!"

Julie began to cry, and Freda insisted to the teller, "We want our money so we can buy our pony."

The teller glared at Rosie. "Madam, can't you restrain your children?"

Rosie gave Gertrude a gentle nudge with her foot, and Gertrude's howls increased.

People began coming in from the street.

"What's the matter with the little girl?" somebody asked.

"The children have twenty-five dollars in this bank they've been saving for a pony, and this man won't let them have it," Rosie explained. "I guess the bank is a little bit shaky."

"Young woman, you can be sued for making false allegations about the condition of a bank!" The teller looked toward the door of Mr. Dahl's office. The door opened and Robert came out. "What's going on here?" He glared at Gertrude. "Who is this little brat?"

"They're my nieces, Bob. They only want their money."

Dahl turned crimson. "For heaven's sake, Rosie, why didn't you come to me instead of causing a riot in here? Carter, give them their money." He stamped back to his office, slammed the door.

Freda eagerly gathered up twenty-five dollars in bills. "Where is the interest?" she asked politely. "Interest at two percent."

Carter's mouth dropped. He counted out thirty-three cents, and the girls threaded their way out.

"I'm glad they got their pony money," the woman called after them.

"Did you have it all planned beforehand, or did it just happen?" a man outside asked.

"It just happened."

"God, it took nerve, either way. I couldn't have done it."

She returned the children to school, and went back to the house to tell Mary.

"Rosie, how could you do it? I'd have given anything to see Bob Dahl's face."

They had coffee and cinnamon rolls, and then Rosie looked at the clock. "I'd better get down to the bus station. If I had the keys I could pick up Hal's car and drive myself back."

"Is Hal's car up here?"

"He had to leave it in some farmer's yard, the snow was too deep with a load on. They caught the train and then they lost their whiskey on a boxcar that was switched, and they had to chase it on a passenger train. It's a wonder they didn't freeze to death."

Mary frowned. "Rosie, how long are you going to put up with Hal?"

"I get furious with him, but all the same—"

"You know what Mama would have said."

"Mama's not here." Rosie gave her sister a hug, put on her coat and her galoshes, and walked to the cigar store where the bus stopped. Riding back in the dark, with the early sharp stars cutting the sky, she thought about Hal, and about the way things were. I ought to have more backbone, she told herself. I ought to fight for a better place to live, and something solid. But Hal is never sure of what he'll clear, and I'm sure I won't have anything left after I buy stockings and shoes for work. Some people are making money—Homer, and that Olsen at the Park Hotel, and the cops that take the payoffs, and even the Prohis. Money isn't it, anyway. It isn't money.

As they pulled into the depot at Minot, she knew she would give anything if Hal were there to meet her, with his strangling hug and his blue blue eyes looking straight into hers.

4

Hal and George and Barney stayed in a cabin camp on the outskirts of Minneapolis the first night. The mattresses were filled with corn husks, and the heat came stingily out of a stinking kerosene stove. Barney wasn't happy with the accommodations.

"Trouble with you, you've always gone home to bed," Hal told him. "You've never slept in a boxcar when it was twenty or thirty below."

"I slept in a boxcar when I ran away that time and went to Spokane. Dad sent you after me, as if I was nothing but a baby."

"You were only fifteen. Why did you run away? You never told us."

"I guess I was tired being at home." Barney held out his big hands to the pale heat. "It was the geraniums, mostly. I don't like geraniums."

"In tin cans all over the place," Hal remembered. "Every windowsill, every table, every shelf. What if Hortense has geraniums?"

"I'll break her neck."

The owner of the camp, a seedy, shifty-eyed character with limp hair and a dirty handkerchief he used frequently, came in to talk. "I'm Griggs. I like to get acquainted with my people, even if they don't stay long." He had stories to tell that nobody wanted to hear.

"Ever hear the poem about the ex-Governor of North Dakota?" They had, but he recited it anyway:

"Forty years ago on the rockbound coast of Norway
A baby boy was born
R. A. Nestes, King of North Dakota . . ."

Hal looked at George, who was staring at the ceiling and whistling.

"R. A. Nestes, King of North Dakota
Twice I have shit in the Governor's chair
And now I come back for the t'ird."

In the middle of the great poem, there was another knock and George let in Walter Simms from the Buick garage in Minot.

"I knew that was your car, Hal."

"You should. You worked on it enough."

"Ever get that bullet hole fixed in the back seat?"

Griggs sat up like a rat smelling cheese.

"You must be thinking of some other car. Draw up a chair and get warm at this beautiful fire we have here."

"You on your way to Stevens Bend?"

"No. Barney has to see a doctor in Minneapolis."

Walter smiled. "You need two cars to get Barney to a doctor? Sure you're not hauling a little something to the parched throats of Minot?"

"Shut up, Walter." Hal glanced at Griggs.

"Don't worry about me." Griggs waved a hand. "They come through here all the time. I'm used to it—in fact, I depend on them for a little nip now and then. But maybe you ain't heard what's goin' on?"

"What is going on?" George looked down a long way to see this creature.

"Hijackers. Out of Minneapolis."

Barney stopped warming his hands.

"Shoot to kill. They don't want nobody getting alcohol from Wisconsin cheaper than they sell it for. They wrecked one guy three different times."

Walter agreed. "They're after anybody hauling from Wisconsin, but I heard if you pay them fifty cents a gallon on your load they let you go."

George said all this was of no interest to three fellows going to see a doctor in Minneapolis.

When Walter and Griggs finally left the cabin, Barney was frightened. "We've got to go back, Hal. I don't want to get shot. I never wanted to come on this damned trip, and I'm not going to get killed before the wedding."

"Wait till after the wedding," George agreed. "You'll enjoy it more."

"Barney, that old man doesn't know anything. He just enjoys shooting the bull. He liked seeing you scared and the whites of your eyes rolling around. We've made this run before and nothing happened. We don't go through Minneapolis, and we watch out for the sheriff at Onoka, that's all. In Wisconsin nobody bothers you."

"Why not?"

"They don't have any state law there on Prohibition. And the Feds look the other way. It's a big moneymaker for the state."

Barney said that was fine, if they only had to drive through Wisconsin, but they had Minnesota and North Dakota, and he didn't like it.

Hal heard Barney turning over during the night on the

crackling mattress. It was very cold in the cabin. Hal got up and put on his sheepskin and his pants and got back in bed. George snored peacefully on a single cot that was too small for him. About five in the morning he fell off with a resounding bump and they all got up, shivered into their clothes, climbed into the stiff leather car seats, and went off to breakfast in an all-night beanery.

"I always thought you fellows lived high when you went on one of these runs," Barney complained. "These are the worst hotcakes I ever ate."

"They're not bad," George told him. "They need a little baking powder, a little shortening, an egg or two, some salt, and maybe ten more minutes on the griddle. But I wouldn't say they're bad."

The Tribune carried a story with pictures of two overturned, burning cars, hijacked near the city the day before. Barney ate no more.

"You will soon be seeing the great city of Minneapolis," George told him. "One damned flour mill after another."

Barney liked the city, the busy smell of it, the trains, the smoke, the signal lights, the whole thing. He thought he and Hortense ought to come here to live someday. Hal couldn't see anything in it—a great big unsorted heap, as bad as Minot.

"With all these Swedes, it's got to be Lutheran," George warned.

"What's wrong with Lutheran? Hortense is a Lutheran."

They were expected in Stevens Bend, and their accommodations were far superior to those of the night before. The sheriff took care of his customers. By three in the morning the load was outside, ready for them: two hundred gallons of 198-proof alcohol, in gallon cans, wrapped three cans together. When Barney saw the car springs sag, he was sure they would be spotted instantly and thrown in jail.

"We won't get picked up," Hal assured him, "and if we do, old Doug Smith will pry us out."

"Who's Smith?"

"He's the lawyer for all of us. He knows exactly what to do."

"I'll bet." Barney rode with Hal, and George followed in the second car. Barney had his arms clamped around his chest, and his jaw was white over his clenched teeth.

"You'll feel better after breakfast," Hal told him.

"When is that?"

"We'll get a few miles behind us, then we'll stop."

It began to break day and they could see the snowy rolling hills, the dark brown-green of winter fir and spruce, the pale bare limbs of cottonwood, the big red barns and the steaming manure piles, the frosty breath of cattle and horses in the barnyards. Hal pointed out things that might take Barney's mind off his situation—camp robbers, sharp royal blue against a pine bough, a weasel, a skunk, a beaver sitting up to listen, a muskrat scrunched down over a tasty root, whiskers twitching.

Barney wasn't listening or looking, so Hal said, "Did you ever think about the names we've tied to perfectly decent birds? Snipe. Shrike. Shidepoke."

"You're going north," Barney said suddenly. "What are you going north for?"

"We can't go through Minneapolis with a load, and we've got to cross the river, so we'll go through Onoka."

"I thought you said the sheriff at Onoka was always on the lookout."

"He is, but it's better than going way up to Duluth.

After we get around Minneapolis, *you* can drive." Barney wasn't sure he wanted to.

They went through a nice clean little town, and Barney said, "There was a good cafe."

"I didn't see it. Never mind, we'll hit another one soon."

Another five miles and Barney said again, "There's a cafe, Hal."

"Wait till we cross the bridge."

Hal could see George coming behind at a steady pace, the Ford riding low in the snowy ruts.

They crossed the river and went through the center of Onoka without meeting any law, and on the outskirts Hal said, "Okay, we'll stop at the first cafe you see, Barney."

Barney sat up like a jackrabbit. "There's one coming up. It's lighted. It's got to be open."

They stopped and George pulled in behind. "We're not really out of Onoka, Hal. You think we should stop now?"

"Barney's half starved. Come on, we'll make it quick."

The place smelled good inside, it was one of those fresh-cream and fresh-egg and lean-bacon places that you hit pretty often in Wisconsin and Minnesota.

Barney ordered bacon and eggs and a stack, and his face was glowing. They all washed up in the good hot water in the washroom.

Barney tasted the syrup, and said it was real maple. "We sure picked the right place, Hal. I'm glad you didn't stop before."

The morning paper from St. Paul lay on the counter, and George, seeing a story about the capture of some rumrunners out of Minneapolis, carefully folded it and put it behind the cash register. Barney, his nose pointed toward the serving window into the kitchen, didn't notice.

Their breakfasts arrived, steaming and golden on hot platters with plenty of fried potatoes. Barney lathered everything with butter, poured on the syrup and took his first bite.

The door opened, letting in the winter and a truck driver. "You fellows belong to those two cars outside?"

Hal nodded.

"I just passed the sheriff down the road and your cars look like his kind of meat."

"Thanks." Hal slid into his coat, put a bill on the cash register. He knew Barney's face would be a painful sight, so he didn't look at it. "Come on," he said.

"You're not leaving?" the girl pleaded. "All that good food—can't I wrap it up for you?"

"No time, thanks very much."

"I want mine wrapped," Barney pleaded, but they each took an arm and lifted him outside and into the car and were off. Hal, looking back, could see the blast of hot exhaust as the sheriff got into gear and roared after them.

Barney huddled down in the seat. "We're in for it now. I might as well have ate my breakfast."

"We won't be caught, Barney. You'll see." Hal turned a corner, sped down two blocks, turned another corner, saw that George was following, and wound in and out of the quiet residential streets hoping the law would get tired.

"Can you see him?" he asked Barney.

"No, but he's after us, Hal."

"He's gone back to the cafe for his coffee. Lawmen hate to miss their coffee." Hal cautiously approached the highway, pulled into it, looked behind him. Not two blocks away, coming at a fast clip, was the sheriff. He gunned it, and Barney scrunched down in the seat. "You can't get away from him, Hal. He's got us now."

"Don't give up, we'll outrun him."

They were doing sixty-five with George close behind. The sheriff turned off, disappeared. Hal was still doing sixty when they came up against a line of slow-moving cars.

"Oh, God," Barney breathed. "We're gone now."

"We'll pass 'em."

"We can't. It's a long line. Maybe twenty cars."

Hal shot out and around, passed three cars and saw a small truck coming toward him. He would have to force his way into the line; whether they liked it or not. A fellow held back, letting him in, either from kindness or fear.

"Now you're stuck in this line and he'll come along and pick you off like a cockroach."

"No, he won't. Look ahead of you, Barney. What do you see?"

"I see us in jail about a thousand miles from home."

"You're not looking. You're so sure we're sunk that you don't see the great piece of luck we've run into. The first car in this line is a hearse. And right ahead of the hearse is a motorcycle cop. We're going to somebody's funeral. Barney. I don't know who he is, but I'm sure grateful to him for getting buried this morning."

"That sheriff will spot you, with this load on, no matter what kind of a procession you're in."

"I'm betting he won't. I'm betting he'll see a funeral procession, and that's all." Hal privately was not so sure. The sheriff could have come around by another route and be waiting for the procession to pass. He could be watching every car in the line. Their springs would give them away. George, having taken in the situation, was bringing up the rear. It wasn't good for him to be the last car, where his North Dakota license would be noticeable.

They had gone about two miles when Hal spotted the sheriff's car, half hidden by a lilac hedge, waiting.

"Oh, God, there he is," Barney cried. "He'll see us sure. If he doesn't see us he'll see George."

"Don't look at him. The way your eyes are bulging he'll know you're a crook."

Hal looked straight ahead at the hat of the woman in the fancy maroon coupe. The hat was small and brown, and had a three-foot pheasant feather sticking up on the side, and the feather bent against the roof. He would remember that hat. His hands were tight and cold in his wool-lined leather gloves. They were almost to the lilac hedge. They were past the hedge. The sheriff's car had not moved. "Look back and see if George made it," Hal ordered.

"I don't see anything going on. I see his car. He's the last in line."

For another three miles they stayed with the procession, then the corpse and the mourners turned off on a gravel road. Hal looked at Barney. "I suppose you're you're going to say you're hungry."

"Why wouldn't I be?"

Their second breakfast was nothing like the first, and Barney pointed that out. To Hal, food was just something that kept you in shape to enjoy other things, but Barney would never get over that beautiful stack of hotcakes he left in Onoka.

They let him drive George's car down through the quiet country of Minnesota, and George rode a few miles with Hal so they could talk. Occasionally you would see where a big barn had burned down, and the still it had harbored was left standing high in the air. The whole country was peppered with stills, coast to coast.

"Do you think Prohibition was a mistake?" George asked.

"Hell, no. How would we make a living in these times without it? Volstead was a prophet—he knew we'd need bootlegging in the country come hard times."

They passed a red barn on which someone had painted:
JESUS SAVES / THE WAGES OF SIN IS DEATH.

"Isn't the wages of anything death?" Hal objected. "How do you get out of death?"

"I can't answer that," George admitted. "Did you ever consider how many useful things we know, Hal? There must be a way to turn all this information into cash."

"What kind of information?"

"Squeaky Simpson soaks his feet in formaldehyde so he won't get athlete's foot."

"Is that right?"

"Unshelled peanuts are bad luck in a whorehouse. If you take a room over an undertaker's establishment you will never be troubled with bedbugs. And speaking of vermin, I wonder how Dick Scott is?"

"Let's not spoil a pleasure trip with thoughts of Dick Scott."

George looked at him thoughtfully. "It's a wonder he has such a nice little girl."

"She's got the nerve and push of her old man. She looks like a kitten, but she's really a gopher."

"I thought you liked her."

"I don't like her or dislike her. I've never had a chance to talk to her, George."

"I wonder what she'd think of you if she knew how you make a living."

Hal thought she must know, her father would have told her all about him. "The kids think it's smart to be seen with us—'look at me, I'm dancing with a real live bootlegger.'"

Things were going along smoothly, the sky was the bright cold blue that went with a late winter's day, they met very few cars and no Feds. Small animals went about their daily chores, chewing and gathering food in the fields of stubble padded with snow. The farmers went about their daily chores of the same kind. They seemed safe enough in bad times, but the fear of losing their land for taxes hung heavy over them.

They drove all night, Barney spelling them off. Toward morning, Hal, driving alone, dozed. He came to with a jolt when George drove up alongside, honking. "You've led us around this same section fence three times, Hal. For God's sake, wake up!"

In Grand Forks they ran into a friend of George's who said he'd heard the Feds were watching the highway coming into Minot from the east. They concluded it would be safer to circle round and come in from the north. George and Barney went on ahead, and Hal waited a while before following them. No use running two cars into a noose.

Hal was coming along at an easy speed across the open prairie when he began to notice a lot of unusual activity on the road. Cars and trucks were tearing up the gravel, passing each other, turning off on side roads, stopping for consultation. This was not good, whatever it meant. He was about to turn into a field and take cover behind a sandhill when another car came out of that field, from behind that sandhill. The fellow in a mackinaw at the wheel looked like a deputy, so Hal backed up and started down the road as fast as the load would permit. The deputy followed, Hal saw he couldn't outrun him so he pulled over.

The first question from that big face under the peak of the plaid cap was where was he heading, and Hal said, "Minot." "And where have you been? Been anywhere near Stanfield this morning?"

"No, I'm on my way back from Minneapolis."

"Transporting illicit beverages?" The face was dark and severe. "From the looks of your springs, you've got a pretty good load on there. If you want to save it, you'd better get the hell off this road. The bank at Stanfield was robbed last night and the whole territory is leaping with law."

Hal thanked him, reached into the back for a can of alcohol. "I'd like to return the favor. Maybe you know a friend of mine from Stanfield. Rosie Robinson."

"Rosie? I sure do. Tell her you saw Pat Kearns." He accepted the can. "She sure caused a sensation in the bank the other day."

"What kind of a sensation?"

"She was smart, Rosie was. I bet Dick Scott wishes he'd got his money out of there."

"Did he have some in the Stanfield bank?"

Kearns smiled. "Must have been a chunk, the way he hollered this morning. We were there, trying to keep some kind of order, but we didn't succeed very well, with all those depositors and everybody that had a lockbox going through the mess on the floor. Papers everywhere. Money everywhere at first, but that didn't last long. Everybody's private affairs spread out for everybody else to see."

Hal said he didn't understand. Why was everything on the floor? Kearns said the robbers used dynamite, and from the results he didn't think they knew much about dynamite.

"They used enough to blow up the courthouse. Anyway, Scott would have massacred Bob Dahl if we'd let him. Sore—man, was he sore!"

"Wonder why he didn't keep his money down in Minot?"

"Search me. Maybe it was friendship. If it was, the friendship is no more." Kearns took his elbow off the hood, started away, came back. "Did you hear somebody took a shot at Boots Cunningham the other night? Shattered the windshield, but didn't hurt him, lucky guy."

"Who was it?"

"He doesn't know. Probably some damned bootlegger."

"He's never been unfriendly—he's immigration, not liquor."

"Maybe somebody didn't know that."

They parted, and Hal made his way down to Minot by the back roads. He kept thinking about Boots. No ordinary rumrunner would take a shot at Boots. He must be onto something a lot more serious than whiskey crossing the line. But what was it?

When he reached the Park Hotel he found Olsen in the dining room with Doug Smith, the lawyer for most of the bootleggers.

"What time did George and Barney get here?" he asked.

Olsen looked at him. "They haven't been here."

Hal had a sinking feeling, but he said he would unload

and probably they'd come along before he was through. They didn't come along, and Olsen grew nervous. It would be hell to lose half the cargo from that run to Wisconsin. Hal told him about the law running all over the roads out of Stanfield because of the bank robbery last night.

"Why the hell were you way up there, when you could have come straight in from Grand Forks?"

"A guy told us it was safer to come in from the north. We didn't know about the bank robbery."

Olsen rubbed his hair and had two more cups of coffee, and then the call came in. Olsen took it. After a couple of minutes he handed the phone to Hal. "The stuff has been confiscated. Your brother wants to talk to you."

"Hal, I'm in jail in Stanfield. You've got to get me out of here. Hortense won't stand for this at all."

"We'll get you out, don't worry. Who's the sheriff? Maybe I know him."

"McGee, his name is. He's a nice fellow, Hal, but I can't be in jail. I've got to be married tomorrow."

"I know, Barney. Just take it easy, help is on the way."

As it turned out, help was not exactly on the way. Olsen was willing to go bail for one of them, but not for two. He chose to make it George, because he reasoned they would let Barney go when they found out he wasn't a bootlegger. Hal argued, but got nowhere.

"Don't worry, Hal, it'll be all right," Smith told him. "We'll have your brother out of there in plenty of time to get married tomorrow. Who's he marrying?"

"Hortense Beirmeister."

Smith didn't see why Barney wanted to get out of a nice safe jail to marry Hortense.

Hal felt uneasy about letting Doug Smith go up to

Stanfield alone to take care of this thing, but he was dog-tired, so he smothered his conscience and went up to his room and fell into bed.

He was asleep when the light snapped on. Rosie came over and looked at him. "When did you get back?"

"Hello, Rosie. Turn off the light."

"I've got to change my dress and go to work. Did you make it all right with the load?"

"I did, but George and Barney got caught. They're in jail in Stanfield. The bank was robbed there last night."

"I heard that. I also heard *you* did it."

"You heard *I* did it!"

"That's what they said. A Buick like yours was in the robbery."

"I was nowhere near Stanfield last night, and I wasn't driving my Buick. You know that."

"I know it. I also know you couldn't rob a bank."

Hal propped himself on both pillows and watched her pull on a clean white slip. "I don't know why you say that. I could if I had to."

"You're not that kind of fellow." Rosie began to wind her side hair around rats.

"Why don't you bob your hair?"

She gave him a look. "If you want a girl with bobbed hair, take up with that Wanda Scott."

"Jealous?" He got up and kissed her on the back of the neck and returned to bed. "Who told you I robbed the bank at Stanfield?"

"Homer said he heard it, I don't know who from."

"I wonder if Scott started it?"

Rosie stopped punishing her hair and turned around. Her eyes were suddenly very dark, very serious. "Hal, you'd better not fool around with that man. You don't know what he might do to you."

Hall heard the clump of galoshes coming up the bare stairs. It was a quick determined step, not heavy. There was no knock—the door flew open and Hortense came through it like birdshot. "Barney's in jail! You thought I wouldn't hear it, didn't you, but I heard it! You've got to get him out right now, the wedding is tomorrow morning."

"Doug Smith's gone up there to get him out, Hortense."

"Doug Smith! He couldn't get a fly out of his own soup."

"He has a law diploma from Harvard University," Rosie put in.

"Harvard!" Hortense spat the word in the direction of the washbasin. "You had no business taking Barney, your own little brother, on one of your rotten bootlegging runs where you knew he could get caught—"

"He did it for you, Hortense. He wanted to make a little extra money for his bride."

Hortense didn't listen. "You robbed the bank at Stanfield, and if you got Barney into that too, you're going to pay for it the rest of your life, Hal Brady."

"Who told you all this?" Rosie demanded, coming between Hortense and the bed.

"Never mind who told me, I know it, and it's the dirtiest lowdown trick you ever pulled, Hal Brady. You ought to be ashamed of yourself, your own brother who never did you any harm, he always looked up to you like you deserved it, you were a hero. Some hero!"

"Sit down, Hortense," Hal pleaded. "Sit down and let me tell you the whole story."

"I heard the whole rotten story, I don't want to hear

any more story. I just want Barney out of jail. Now. This minute."

"Give them time to get back. Stanfield's forty miles from here."

"Why the hell should Barney be the one to go to jail, and you lying here like a king in your own bed? Barney never did anything illegal in his whole damned life."

"You're swearing, Hortense."

"I'll do more than that, Hal Brady, if you don't get Barney down here for his wedding tomorrow." Hortense stood now in the center of the room waving her long thin arms in their worn brown wool sleeves. It wasn't much of a coat she had, the velvet collar was threadbare and the hem was uneven. Hal felt a sudden pinch of pity for Hortense, so fiercely loyal to Barney.

Rosie was just plain mad. "Barney didn't have to go along on this trip. He wanted the money, so he went. Hal isn't to blame for that."

"Hal talked him into it. He's got to get up and do something right now. Barney's sleeping on the cold cement floor with lice all over him in the Stanfield jail."

"No, Hortense," Hal protested. "Doug Smith and Barney are probably on their way back right now. Maybe Barney is at your house, wondering where you are."

Suddenly Hortense began to cry, and Rosie changed sides. "Hal, are you sure he's getting out? Are you sure he had bail?"

Hal folded back the covers, put his feet on the floor. "You women won't let a man get any rest. I'll go down and see Olsen again, Hortense, if you'll get out of here so I can get dressed."

"You'd better!" She flung open the door and went clumping down the stairs.

"Were you telling the truth? Do you believe Barney's out?" Rosie demanded.

"I had to make it sound good for Hortense, didn't I?"

"I worried about you, Hal."

"Why? Nothing happened. We had a real good run until George met up with the law. I have a hunch he was delivering a can of alcohol to a friend of his out of Stanfield. He has all kinds of friends and he wants to be good to them."

"Something like you. Neither one of you ever thinks about the people really close to you, it's just these casual friends you want to do big generous favors for. Want to hear how I made out with the girls at the bank?"

"I heard the girls got their money. How did you manage that?"

"I told Gertrude to lie on the floor and scream till they let go of the money."

"You told her to scream—in the bank?"

Rosie laughed. "You're shocked. You're actually shocked. A man who thinks nothing of hauling booze from Wisconsin to North Dakota with the law shooting at him all the way, gets prickly heat when a little girl makes a fuss in a bank."

"I don't think that's so funny."

"I do. I think for you a bank is a church."

He was indignant. "I hate banks."

He let Rosie off at the Prairie Dog and went on over to the Park Hotel. He still had Olsen's car, and he'd have to go up to Stanfield and get the Buick. Olsen was at a table in the downstairs dance hall, thinking on paper napkins. He had maps of future enterprises drawn out, and his small blue eyes were not seeing any of the crowd in the joint; they were seeing roads and hills and border hoppers and loaded springs in his two Fords. Hal asked how Doug Smith had made out in Stanfield.

"I haven't seen him yet, Brady. He'll do the best he can."

"I told you Barney is figuring on getting married tomorrow."

"Yeah, you told me that. A man can get married anytime, Hal."

Hal explained that Hortense had the church waiting to jump for this wedding, that the cakes would spoil, the bridesmaids grow old and wrinkled if Barney had to stay in jail another week.

"Why does a hasher have to have a wedding like that? She should be satisfied with a justice of the peace."

Hal frowned. The same idea had been in his mind, but when Olsen stated it that way, without any feeling or understanding, it angered him. "She doesn't want to be a hasher all her life. This is part of something bigger—" Hal stopped. Olsen wasn't listening, and he probably wouldn't understand if he did listen. He was a man with one purpose—making as much as he could out of the Volstead Act before repeal. Repeal was in the wind—it wouldn't come under Hoover, but it was coming. A man had to concentrate.

Hal turned around, and there was George Finley.

"Where's Barney?" Hal demanded.

"They wouldn't let him go. I didn't like to leave without him, but I wasn't doing him any good there and I thought maybe I could do something down here. How about it, Olsen?"

Olsen waved a long arm. "Stop worrying. They'll let him go."

Hal wanted to know what kind of jail it was, dirty and

lousy, or clean, and was the food all right. George said it was a very nice jail, as jails went. The beds were clean, if hard, and the food was plentiful. "I'm not saying they know how to cook, but it's good food before they tackle it."

George and Hal moved away from Olsen. There was nothing more to be got out of him.

"If Barney is still locked up tomorrow morning, I'll have to tell Hortense to postpone the wedding," Hal decided.

"Maybe you ought to tell her tonight."

"There's still a chance he might get out in time."

George shook his head. "You know there isn't."

"Let's pretend there is. I couldn't face Hortense again so soon."

"Did you hear that somebody tried to kill Boots the other night?" George asked.

"I heard. What do you think is going on?"

"I don't know, but I don't like it, Hal."

Hawk came along. "I hear Barney's getting married tomorrow."

"He was, but right now he's in the Stanfield jail."

Hawk looked puzzled. "Don't Hortense know it?"

"She knows it."

"And she ain't got him out? I thought Hortense could bust open a jail with one hand. Would it be okay for me to go to the wedding, when they have it?"

"Sure, Hawk, you can go. You're an old friend."

"Thanks. I sure wouldn't want to miss Barney's wedding."

When Hal got back there was a message for him in Toni Murphy's downstairs. "This girl phoned and asked for you, and I said, 'Who is it, can I give him a message?'

and she said, 'It's Wanda and tell him to phone me Sunday at my house.' Who is Wanda, Hal?"

"I don't know. Never heard of her. Thanks for the message, though."

"You must of heard of her. She knows you."

"All the girls know me, Toni."

Hal went upstairs. What was the matter with Wanda Scott, anyway? Did she want to get him killed by her own father? He took off his shirt, and one shoe, and sat there thinking.

Then he wrote himself a note:

Sunday
Go to Barney's Wedding
Don't go to Barney's Wedding
Call Wanda

He stuck the note in the mirror, went to bed. He had been asleep for some time when Rosie snapped on the light.

She tiptoed around, shedding her clothes, putting on a pair of lumpy knitted bed socks, her black chiffon nightgown, her toilet paper curlers. Finally she went over to the basin, looked in the mirror, examined one eyelid closely. Then she saw the note. She was a fast reader. She snatched the water glass from the tin holder beside the basin.

Hal ducked in time. "Come here, Rosie. Let me pat your fat little behind."

She didn't move.

"Come on, I put the note there for you to read. I like to see you throw things."

She came over, suspicious but wanting to believe him. "You're going to call her and take her out."

"You know I wouldn't take a girl out on Sunday. Too dead. No fun." He tied a knot in the ribbon that went round her nightgown. "I'm glad you're fat. I don't like skinny girls."

"I'm not fat! I'm healthy. That Scott girl is a skeleton, and her teeth stick out like a mule deer." Rosie handed him the alarm clock. "Fix it to go off at eight-fifteen. I want to be down at Tolefson's at nine o'clock so I won't miss anything."

"Tolefson's isn't open on Sunday."

"It is this Sunday. They're having a big sale."

"What are you planning to buy?"

"A toaster, so we can have toast with our coffee when we get up." Rosie got into bed and put her cold little bottom against him, and he hugged her till she got warm and went to sleep. Then he lay there thinking. He had to go to Stanfield to get the Buick tomorrow or Monday, and when he did he would run up to Portal and see Boots and find out what was going on. Maybe Boots himself didn't know who had tried to kill him. But maybe he did know—he was certainly brooding over something when they saw him on their run to Estavan.

Suddenly Rosie sat up in bed. "Hal, this is a terrible way to live."

"What's wrong with the way we live?"

"We only have one room."

"How many rooms do you want?"

"Two."

"But you can only be in one room at a time, Rosie."

5

Early in the morning, it couldn't have been more than nine-thirty, Mrs. Murphy pounded on the door. "Hal, you're wanted on the phone!" She only had to say it once, Ada Murphy had a voice like a train wreck.

Hal went down in his bare feet and his coat, wondering what terrible thing had happened to make anybody call at this hour. It was Hortense. "Barney didn't come back. You didn't do a damned thing last night, did you?"

"Let me get my breath, Hortense."

"You could of told me last night he wouldn't be here, and I could of let everybody know, and now I've got to tell the minister to cancel everything at the last minute, with the flowers in the church and the wedding cake here and the sandwiches all made, and Dad even took a bath. You make me sick, Hal Brady!" She banged the phone.

Hal got dressed and went down to the Park Hotel. Olsen said Doug Smith was really working on the case, but there wasn't anything he could do on Sunday, the sheriff wasn't on duty, just a deputy. "Don't worry, we'll get Barney out."

Hal had very little confidence in Doug Smith. He would go up to Larsen's in the morning and get the Buick, and then go into Stanfield and talk to the sheriff.

When he got back to the room, Rosie was there. She was sitting in a big blue velvet chair with her hat and coat on. She looked like a cat full of mouse. "Isn't it beautiful?"

"It's a funny shape for a toaster."

"The toasters were only marked down a dollar, Hal, and this was half price. All I have to pay is two dollars a week."

"Rosie, you're crazy. How did you get it delivered so fast?"

"Hawk brought it up for me in his truck."

"It looks like hell in this room."

"We aren't going to live here forever."

He gave her a funny look. "If you like it, honey, it's fine. I've got to go now. You'd better take a nap. You were up before the chickens."

Rosie watched him throw on his jacket, listened to his firm, confident tread on the stairs going down. He generally left when she mentioned any sort of change, any sort of claim on him. She stood there looking at the new chair, and all the fun had gone out of it.

The next morning Barney was still in jail. Hal picked up George at Sullivan's and they set off to get the Buick and try to pry Barney loose.

They stopped first at Larsen's.

"Hello, Brady. Come in, come in." Fred Larsen's smile was almost too broad, too shiny, as he let them into the big kitchen.

"I guess you thought we'd never come for the car," Hal said. "We had to make a business trip."

Mrs. Larsen served coffee and rolls and some crsip flatbread she had just made. She hovered in the background, and Hal felt she didn't want them there in the kitchen.

"I hear they think I robbed the bank in Stanfield," Hal said.

That touched a nerve in Larsen—he tightened up, his blue eyes narrowed. "They don't know who did it, Brady. There's a lot of talk."

"You know I didn't do it in my car. The car was right here all the time. You could tell them that."

Mrs. Larsen opened her mouth. Her husband gave her a look. He did the talking. "I don't like to say, right out, that I let a bootlegger leave his car in my barnyard. I did you a favor, and I was glad to do it, Brady, but to advertise it to all the neighbors—you know, there's people don't think what you boys are doing is exactly the right thing to be doing, and it gives a man a bad name around the country, and I don't want my family to suffer for it. Do you see what I mean?"

George was studying the contents of his coffee cup.

Hal said, "Sure, Larsen, I understand that. You wouldn't want to get into a tight place over this."

"I don't mean I wouldn't help you if you got to the point of going to the pen, but until it comes to that, I would rather stay out of it."

"Sure, sure. We get the idea. I hope I won't have to call on you. What's the sheriff like?"

Larsen was happy to get off the central subject. "He's a good fellow, a very good fellow. They're sure keeping him busy. The bank robbery Friday night, and last night that customs man ran off the road and killed himself."

"What customs man?"

"What was his name, Myrtle?"

"Cunningham," Mrs. Larsen said. "Didn't you hear about it down in Minot?"

"No, we didn't hear about it," Hal told her, feeling suddenly not hungry. "Thank you for the rolls and coffee."

Outside, George said, "What do you think of that?"

"It's a damned shame, and I wonder if it was an accident."

"I wish he'd told us what was on his mind that day."

Hal got into the Buick and it started with remarkable ease for a car that hadn't been used for almost a week. George took Olsen's car and they went on into Stanfield to the courthouse.

Gordon McGee was a good-natured fellow, well-built, plenty of muscle, able to hold his own in a fight, but not likely to engage in one unless it was absolutely necessary. He was wearing a plaid wool shirt and heavy boots, and the laces were fastened the way a lumberjack fastened them, so they wouldn't catch in the brush.

"What can I do for you?" he asked.

"I'm Hal Brady, and I'd like to see my brother."

McGee grinned. "I'm Gordon McGee, and I ought to arrest you, Brady. You're our prime suspect in the bank robbery. What kind of a car do you drive?"

"A dark-blue Buick, license number 857."

"That's the car seen by witnesses at the back of the bank Friday night."

"There are plenty of people who can swear I wasn't anywhere near Stanfield when the bank was robbed. *If* it was robbed."

"If it was robbed? What does that mean?"

"It was shaky, everybody knew that. Maybe it was a convenient thing to let somebody in the back door and carry out what cash they had left. Anyway, I had nothing to do with it, and I'd like to see my brother."

The sheriff wanted to know where he had parked his car, and Hal told him it was out back.

"You put me in a hell of a spot, Brady. Somebody's liable to come along and see that car, and they'll want to know why I don't arrest you."

"You know Fred Larsen at Larsen's Crossing? I left my car at his place while I took a run to Wisconsin last week. He doesn't want people to hear about it, but he will back me up if he has to. The car that robbed the bank must have been some other Buick, McGee."

At that moment Barney came walking down the hall with a cup of coffee. "Am I glad to see you, Hal! When do I get out? You better make it soon or Hortense will kill both of us."

"The sheriff doesn't want to let you out, he wants to put me in."

"What for?"

"Robbing the Stanfield bank Friday night."

"But you weren't here Friday night, we were all in Minnesota or someplace. Weren't we, George?"

George nodded. He had taken one of the armchairs along the wall. "It doesn't seem quite right to arrest a man for a robbery he couldn't have committed."

McGee looked unhappy. "I'm inclined to believe you, Brady, but I wish you had somebody besides your brother and your friend here to swear to it."

"Your deputy, Pat Kearns, was out beating the brush for bank robbers Saturday morning, and he warned me to take my load into Minot by the back roads. He knows I was too busy to rob a bank Friday night."

"I'll phone him at home." McGee got through to Kearns, there was a short conversation, and then he hung up, frowning. "Kearns doesn't remember anything about it, Brady. You sure you saw him Saturday morning?"

"The son of a bitch. Of course I saw him."

"He's probably playing it safe with me. He's new on the force. But this leaves us without any real evidence in your favor. People around here are going to ask me why I don't pick you up."

Hal said he thought the evidence would turn up, but right now he had to take Barney down to Minot so he could get married.

"All right, you can take your brother and get out of here, if you give me your word you won't leave the state."

"You have my word."

"We heard Boots Cunningham got himself killed last night. What happened?" George asked.

"He ran off the road. Car turned over and rolled down the bank. You know where you cross that deep gully on the way to Portal? The road was icy, he could have hit the bridge, we don't know."

"Did somebody take a shot at Boots the other night, or was that just a wild rumor?"

"No, it happened. And we thought of foul play this time but there wasn't any evidence of it. He had bruises, but he got those, we figure, from rolling over the bank."

"Nobody would have a reason to kill Boots, anyway," Hal said. "It's too bad. He was a friend of mine."

McGee nodded. "He was a good guy. A very good guy."

"Did they bring his car in?"

"Walt's garage is going to haul it in."

The three walked out the back door of the courthouse,

and Hal said he would like to see Boots's car. Barney protested. "I've got to get back to Minot, Hal!"

"You'll get back. Let's find Walt's garage."

Walt hadn't had a chance to go after the car yet. "Did you want to get some of the parts or something?"

"No, I just wanted to see the car," Hal told him. "It's hard to believe he ran off the road, he never went over thirty-five miles an hour."

Walt agreed. "Beats me. I'm going up there right now, if you want to follow along."

Barney groaned. "What can you find out from looking at the car?"

Hal didn't really hear Barney, he was thinking about tires. The found Boots's Chevy at the bottom of the gully, on its top. One wheel was gone.

"What do you know," Walt said. "Some damned thief's been here already."

"Wonder why he took only one wheel?" George asked.

"That's all he needed." Walt got busy with cable.

Hal looked inside the car, didn't find anything but snow and broken glass and Boots's old Stetson hat. The hat made him feel bad. "I'm going up to Portal to see his wife."

"For God's sake, Hal," Barney groaned.

"It won't take long."

They were about half an hour up the road to Portal when Hal pulled over and signaled George to stop. "George, if you shot somebody's rear tire and they went off the road, and got killed, would you just leave the tire on the car?"

"I don't know. I might be afraid somebody would catch me removing it."

"You could just say you saw the wreck and climbed down to see if you could help whoever it was."

George said that was possible. "But if somebody shot Boots's tire and then took the wheel off, what would he do with it?"

"He'd hide it someplace."

"Just roll it off the side of the road on his way home?"

"I'd hide it near where the car landed, at the bottom of the gully."

"Too risky," George objected. "Somebody would be sure to find it."

"We didn't. The sheriff didn't."

"That's because it isn't there."

"Want to bet?" Hal turned the Buick and went back, and George followed. Walt had got the car out and was gone.

Barney sat like a stone in the car while Hal and George scrambled down into the gully again and began a methodical search.

The snow had blown off, and George said that was too bad, they could have seen his tracks easily in snow. "But then, he wouldn't have hidden it here, if there had been snow."

After about twenty minutes George called, "Here it is, and the tire's flat."

"Think there's a bullet in it?"

"I'm sure there's a bullet in it."

They pushed the wheel up to the road, Hal got out his iron and they removed the tire. The slug was inside the tube.

Barney got out and looked. "Somebody was sure after him."

They went on to Portal, found Boots's house.

Don't Wake Me Up While I'm Driving

Bess Cunningham had company, a couple of neighbors trying to console her, and she took Hal into the kitchen to talk.

"Do you have any idea where Boots was going last night, Bess?"

She shook her head. She was a small, freckled, red-haired woman, shrewd but kind. "He got a phone call, and he said he had to help a fellow with a job. I naturally thought it had something to do with liquor—that wasn't his job, really, he was immigration, but you know how mixed up things have got in the last few years."

"He got a phone call?"

"Yes, about nine o'clock. He hated to drive after dark. I guess he didn't see that narrow old bridge where he hit the concrete. That's what they think, anyway." She hesitated. "Would you like some coffee, Hal? Cake? Pie? The place is full of food—neighbors being kind. I wonder why people think you're going to eat like a horse when somebody dies. You know, Hal, I keep thinking, Why didn't the man he went out to help with whatever it was, call me when he knew Boots got killed? I haven't heard a word from the bastard. The least he could do is say he's sorry."

"Was anybody sore at Boots—I mean really mad?"

"Nobody ever stayed mad at Boots. How could they? He was the most decent, honest, kind-hearted—" She swallowed hard.

Hal put an arm around her. "I know, Bess. But there were things he had to do in his work that might make people a little bit resentful. He was telling us about confiscating a still a few days ago."

"Tom O'Connor's still? Sure, he did that for Mrs. O'Connor. I guess Tom was pretty hot about it." She stopped. "You're really asking me if I know anybody who might want to kill him."

"You're right."

"Why?"

"George and Barney and I were just down in that gully looking at Boots's car. There was a bullet in one of the rear tires."

Her eyes got very round, he could see the tiny red veins around the deep-blue iris. "What does that mean?"

"I think it means somebody called him up and invited him to come out and get killed."

"My God!" She sat down suddenly. "You think somebody shot one of his tires to make him go off the road?"

Hal nodded. "I wouldn't say anything about it. Let the son of a bitch think nobody found the bullet."

"But who would want to kill Boots?"

"When we came through here not long ago, Bess, I thought he had something on his mind. You don't know what it was?"

She agreed that Boots had seemed worried, but he hadn't told her why.

Barney didn't protest when Hal said he was taking a quick run out to Tom O'Connor's place. Barney had concluded it was hopeless to try to stop him, and besides he was beginning to take an interest in the way things were developing.

Tom was at home, huddled by the stove in his slab shack, mourning over the devastation Boots had caused when he took all his equipment for making moon. Mrs. O'Connor swept a couple of kids and some dirty underwear off three chairs and asked them to sit down.

"It's too bad about Boots Cunningham," she said. "I sure liked that man."

"Son of a bitch," Tom growled. "Son of a bitch."

"He only done it for your good, Tom."

"He ruined me. You know what that still cost me?"

"It didn't cost you nothin', you got it free from Sammy."

"I paid Sammy off in booze, you know I did. Say, Brady, ain't you a bootlegger? You want to buy some first-class stuff?"

Hal said he might. He followed O'Connor down the hill to a shed, watched him take up a couple of floor-boards and pull out his gallon jugs. There was a mouse in one jug.

"Taste it. The best. Thirty dollars for the lot."

Hal didn't taste it, but he took out thirty. "Do you know anybody that would be mad or scared enough to kill Boots Cunningham?"

"Kill him?" O'Connor's scruffy whiskered face showed real surprise. "Hell, no. Everybody liked Boots. I liked him except for breakin' up my still."

They drove away, and Hal said he didn't think O'Connor had anything to do with the wreck. "Now we've just got one more short stop."

"One more stop!" Barney exploded.

"You wouldn't want your brother to be charged with stealing the evidence from the scene of a crime, Barney. I've got to take this bullet to the sheriff."

McGee accepted the bullet with some surprise. "It doesn't look like an accident now, does it, Brady?"

"His wife says somebody called him just before he left last night. She thought it was business."

"Some damned bootlegger."

"What did the coroner have to say?"

"He said, 'The man is dead.' You want to talk to him?

He's up on the second floor. Wait, I'll go with you. I've got some evidence from the bank robbery to give to the clerk of the court. My vault's getting full."

The sheriff unlocked his vault, picked up a couple of cardboard cartons, and they went up the broad stairs to the clerk's office. Mrs. Crane, a prim little woman in gold-rimmed spectacles, accepted the boxes and gave McGee a receipt. "It isn't regular, you know, Sheriff. You should keep these till they're introduced at the trial."

"Right, Helen, but the stuff is safer up here, you never know when a deputy is going to forget and leave our vault open."

He took George and Hal across the hall and introduced them to Jay Proctor, the coroner. "Brady's the guy that donated that load of alcohol, Jay."

Proctor said it had been very good stuff and they all appreciated it. "I wish I had something decent to offer you in return, Brady, but all I've got is what I make myself. I don't recommend it." He opened a big black safe painted with morning glories and took out a case containing several brown bottles.

"That's his embalming fluid," McGee explained, and then he left.

Hal understood Proctor was also the undertaker—the coroner usually was. "What we came to see you about, Mr. Proctor, was Boots Cunningham. Did you find any marks on the body that could indicate he was attacked?"

Proctor looked suddenly grave. "No. What makes you ask?"

They told him about the bullet, while Jay poured three tin cups of milky-brown fluid. Hal's cup had a fly in it.

"I knew Boots well." Proctor made a face as he took a swallow of his own product. "One of the best. Solid as a brick privy. I don't think a bootlegger would try to knock him off. No reason to."

"Who else, then?" George asked.

Proctor shook his head. "You got me." He offered them another drink, but they both refused. Hal wondered if he would survive the first one, his head felt open at the top.

6

When Hal and Barney and George walked into Sullivan's about an hour later, Hortense was speeding through the swinging doors from the kitchen with a trayful of soup bowls. She dropped the tray.

"Barney!" she cried, and ran to him.

Barney looked sheepish as she flung her arms around him, but he was happy too.

"Are you out for good? Is it all right?"

"Sure," Barney told her. "Everything is fine."

"Then the wedding is Sunday."

"Are we invited?" George asked.

"I guess I can't say no. But don't bring any of your drunken friends. No bottles, no drinking. This is going to be a nice wedding."

Hal nodded. "We'll try to be gentlemen, won't we, George?"

"Certainly," George agreed. "It's her first wedding."

"What do you mean, my first wedding? I'm only going to have one wedding. Barney, you go tell the Reverend Grimsrud it's this Sunday at our house, and then go see if you still have your job at Hayden's Grocery, and if he says no I'll see him myself. I know you're all right with G.N. because I checked with them this morning."

"I thought I'd give up that callboy job, Hortense," Barney told her.

"You've already given it up. They're putting you on in the yard as soon as Bert Shilling moves up—that should be sometime this month."

Barney blinked. "How do you know?"

"I talked to the yardmaster."

Hal, watching the two of them, saw how it was going to be for Barney.

Hortense was looking at Barney's pants. "Did you wear your good clothes to jail?" she demanded. "You've got to have a new suit for the wedding. Go over to Nickie's and have him measure you right now."

"Nickie can't make me a suit for this Sunday."

"Of course he can. Tell him you have to have it by Saturday noon."

"How am I going to pay for a new suit?"

"I have enough saved for a down payment."

The three of them walked down the street to Nickie's, and he measured Barney. "He has to have it by Saturday morning," Hal said firmly.

"Saturday morning! Are you crazy? A good suit takes two weeks."

"Just drop everything else and work on Barney's suit. He's getting married Sunday."

"It's impossible." Nickie picked up his tape measure. "But I'll do it."

Hal decided to try to sell O'Connor's moonshine to Mae Monroe, who ran the House where Violet worked.

Mae Monroe was a large, well-muscled woman with a deep voice and a hard eye. "Sure, I'll take your load, if it's good stuff and it ain't too damned high."

"It's not good stuff and it is too damned high."

"Bring in a jug. I don't buy anything sight unseen from you or anybody else, Brady."

Hal brought in a jug. "Hundred and fifty proof."

She took off the cap, sniffed, tasted. "What's it made from?"

"I don't know, but whatever it is, it's dead."

"What do you want for it?"

"I've got to have eighty-five dollars for the nine gallons."

"What did you give for it?"

"Never mind. I had the risk of bringing it through and into town."

"Business isn't so good, Hal. Things are slowing up. I don't know what we're gonna be faced with here."

He smiled and waited, and pretty soon Mae dug down into her giant handbag, came out with a roll and peeled off sixty-five dollars. "You heard what they're trying to do to us? They want every girl to prove she has a legitimate job. How the hell can we do that, Hal? Those damned bastards on the police force, they want to get their paws on every penny I make. How am I gonna have my girls legally employed, I ask you?" After a while she got up the additional twenty.

George had taken no part in these negotiations, but had sat quietly studying a pine-needle pillow on a red plush couch. As he was leaving he turned to Mae. "I have a suggestion for getting around the law."

Her sharp eyes were wary. "Like what?"

"Have a sewing machine for each girl, or maybe each two girls, and when the cops raid they are sitting here industriously sewing baby bonnets."

She started to laugh, and then she got to thinking. They left her thinking.

Hal and George decided they should get new suits for Barney's wedding. They walked over to Monkey Ward's and tried some on. Hal didn't like George in his, and George thought Hal looked like a freshly hatched card shark. They were pulling on their own comfortably worn pants when High Ass Swede came wandering through, turning over the neat piles of shirts and socks, and getting a mean eye from a lady clerk.

"Hal, what you doin' in here?"

"We were thinking about new suits for my brother's wedding Sunday, but the price is too high. I think I'll get a new necktie."

High Ass was shocked. "You don't wanna buy a suit, Hal. Wait till the Boosters get here. They're on their way from Fargo. They should be in anytime now."

The lady clerk moved nearer, listening.

"They can get you your right size and everything."

"There's not much time," Hal objected.

"How much time does it take to steal a suit?"

When Hal told Rosie, she was almost as excited as Hortense at the news that Barney was out of jail and about to be married. He told her about Boots Cunningham, and the bullet in the tire.

"Do you think it was a bootlegger?"

"No, I don't. I think he was onto something else."

She was sitting on her velvet chair, pulling on her stockings. Her smooth forehead took on wrinkles. "If they killed Boots for nosing into this thing, whatever it is, will they like it if you start poking around?"

"I'm not poking around. I just wanted to see if Boots died in an accident, or because somebody wanted him out of the way."

"You watch out, Hal Brady. You don't know what kind of people they are, they may be too much for you."

Hal grinned. "An old rumrunner like me?"

She stepped into her black pumps. "Frenchy wants to see you. He said it was important. And Olsen has a proposition for you, something very good."

Hal didn't know if he wanted to go back to Wisconsin right away. Rosie didn't think it was that. "I'll ride out to Frenchy's with you."

"Okay, we'll stop at the Park and see Olsen first."

Olsen didn't want to talk in front of Rosie. He and Hal went into his office off the hotel lobby. "This is something really good, Hal. An automobile dealer thought it up. We steal two of his new cars, take them across the line, trade one for a load of good whiskey. He collects the insurance on the stolen car, we pay him a percentage of our profits from the liquor, and everybody is happy."

Hal looked blank. "Why does he want his cars stolen?"

"Have you heard of anybody buying a Chrysler lately and paying for it?"

"Where is his dealership?"

Olsen said he wasn't free to give details. It might get out, and then the insurance angle would fall through.

"He's taking a big risk."

"You know what the companies are doing to the dealers? They're busting them. The dealers have a lot of cars sold on time, the buyers can't pay, and the dealer has to make good on them. Why do you think they're all going broke? The risk this fellow would be taking with us isn't equal to the risk of losing his business."

"I'm already accused of robbing a bank. Now you want me to steal automobiles."

"We know you didn't rob that bank, Hal. And this isn't really stealing. The man wants us to take these cars."

"Maybe the man does, but what does the insurance company want? And what about the guys in Detroit?"

"You're splitting hairs. This is a smart, legitimate operation. You think it over, you'll see how good it is. You can give me your answer in a couple of days, but don't wait any longer than that. There are other fellows ready to grab this chance."

"Let them grab it, Olsen."

"No, I want you, if you'll do it. I can trust you." Olsen took out his wallet and started to extract some bills.

"What's that for?"

"A little advance—"

"No. I can tell you right now I won't do it."

"Hal, you're too impulsive. Give this thing some thought. Consider all the angles."

Hal smiled. "I'm not impulsive. But when I see a coiled rattlesnake I jump."

"I don't understand you. Rum-running is against the law."

"I know. But that's different."

"How is it different?"

"To me it's different. I can't explain why. Thanks anyway for offering me the chance, and I'm sorry I can't take it."

"What was the proposition?" Rosie asked as they started out to Frenchy's.

"Olsen has a scheme to steal cars for a dealer and trade them across the line for booze."

"Great. Did you say no?"

"I said no."

Rosie opened the glove compartment, looking for

candy bars. Something pink and silky fell out. She held up a pair of step-ins. "I ought to wrap these around your neck, Hal Brady."

"I never saw them before."

"They're Wanda Scott's and you know it."

"If they're Wanda's she was out with some other fellow in my car. Believe me, honey, I don't know how those pants got into the glove compartment."

They drove into Frenchy's yard, where chickens and bantam hens and a couple of pigs scattered in front of the car and a sad springer spaniel watched them from the back steps. Frenchy came to the door.

"I hear you want to see me," Hal said.

"Yes. Come on in."

Hal was surprised to find the kitchen as clean and neat as a dentist's office, with a smell of baking bread. He'd expected the smell to be of ripe underwear and working mash. Frenchy served coffee and came to the point.

"I think you and me should go into the retail end of this business, Brady. Open up a little place where we can serve my product, and also some good Canadian whiskey which you will bring across. How about it?"

Hal was surprised. Bad offers were coming in from all over. "I don't think so, Frenchy. I'd rather stay in the shipping end of the business. Let somebody else handle the poor devils who drink our stuff."

"Maybe you want a little time to think it over. I've got a couple of locations in mind, cheap rent."

Hal shook his head. "You know how many speakeasies there are. All over town. A party in a different house every night. The competition is too tough."

Rosie spoke up. "I think you should do it, Hal. Frenchy's right, you should be getting more out of it, with all the chances you take. Who gets the hog's share? Olsen. I'll help you—I'm a pretty good barmaid."

"You're a beautiful barmaid, hon." Hal could see the springer looking at him through the porch window. "I sure appreciate the thought, Frenchy, but I'm not your man. When you two are ready, I'll be outside."

"He's going out to steal your dog, Frenchy," Rosie told him.

Hal and the dog walked across the yard, went through a fence and into a field of stubble where a couple of crows were busy. The dog didn't look at the crows, but when they came on a couple of early mallards feeding at the edge of a pond, he was electric with excitement, looking up at Hal for action. "Sorry, fellah, I haven't got my gun." Hal rumpled his ears, found wads of matted hair behind the ears. "I don't get to hunt because I'm tangled up in the liquor business, and you don't get to hunt because you belong to Frenchy, and he's in the same business, and damn it, this is no life for dog or man."

The dog sat back and regarded him soberly, ears lifting and drooping, tail going.

Rosie called from the house, and the two went back.

"You tryin' to steal my dog?" Frenchy asked.

"I'd like to. What would you take for him?"

"Hal, for God's sake," Rosie pleaded. "Where would you keep a dog?"

Frenchy looked at the springer as if he hadn't seen him for a long time, as indeed he probably hadn't, and then he said, "If you want him, you can have him. My brother left him here when he went to the Coast to look for work. He'll never come and get him. It's been three years."

"Hal was just kidding," Rosie told him. "He has no time for a dog."

"I'd make time for this dog," Hal said, and the dog

leaned against him and looked worried. "What's his name?"

"I call him Boy."

"Don't give him to anybody else, Frenchy. I'm coming back for him." The dog followed the car to the gate, and then sat down, watching Hal go away.

Rosie looked back. "He is a good dog, Hal. Why don't we rent a house, so you can keep him?"

"We can't afford a house, and you know it."

"Hortense and Barney are going to have a flat."

"It's a pretty mangy flat, with the paint peeling off the walls and a leaky toilet tank."

Rosie didn't say any more.

Hal looked at her out of the corner of his eye. "You need a new coat more than we need a house."

"I'd rather have a house."

After a minute he said, "I'm going to run up to Stanfield again in the morning."

"What for?"

"It's a matter of some pink silk pants."

Hal dropped Rosie off at the Prairie Dog and went on to the Park Hotel, where he found George. The place was quiet, and George said Olsen was pouring a very bad grade of rye tonight.

"Let's take a run out to the Red Lantern," Hal suggested.

"Do you think Rosie would like that?"

"Why not?"

"All you can do out there is dance with some other girl or girls."

"Rosie doesn't think anything of it if I have a dance or two, or a drink or two, with some other girl. She knows it doesn't mean anything."

"Does she?"

Hal looked at him, surprised. George shrugged, and said, "Come on, then, let's go."

At the Red Lantern, a huge old potato warehouse now used for dances, they found a good crowd and a loud band.

They hadn't been there long when Wanda Scott came in with her friend Woodrow. He looked uncomfortable, but Wanda's cute little face, bright and interested, turned here and there, taking it all in like a farmer at a fair. She had on a light blue coat with a squirrel collar and a little squirrel hat with a bow—too dressy for the Red Lantern.

She saw Hal and came over. Woodrow followed slowly. "Woodrow didn't want to come. He's afraid of a raid. But I love it. The music sounds like a horse stamping on a tin roof. Could we sit with you two?"

"Certainly." Hal caught the barmaid going by. "Two more when you have a chance."

"I think we'd better find a table, Wanda," Woodrow muttered, not looking directly at Hal, but giving the impression of a dog who is beginning to curl his lip.

"Woodrow's always afraid of being a nuisance," Wanda explained. "Hal doesn't mind, really."

"We're glad to have you," Hal assured them, "but it is a rough place for a girl like you, Wanda."

"What kind of a girl do you see me as?"

"I see you as a nice little girl who doesn't know yet what it's all about."

"There's not much fun in being a nice little girl. I mean to correct that as soon as possible."

Her friend drew out another subject, quickly. "Have they caught the man who robbed the Stanfield bank?"

"Not yet," George put in, seeing that the conversation might take a nasty turn. "I wouldn't be surprised if the directors sort of salvaged the money themselves. The story around town was that it was going broke any day."

"That wasn't what I heard. I heard they suspected Hal Brady."

"That isn't nice, Woodrow," Wanda protested. "If Mr. Brady was a suspect he'd be in jail, and he is sitting here free as a bird."

"All the beds in the jail are full," Hal told her.

"Did you get my message? Why didn't you call me?"

"Because I make it my business to protect nice young girls from wicked old men like me."

George was getting bored with it. He got up and left.

"Maybe the girls don't want to be protected."

The barmaid came with the mickeys. "How's Rosie, Hal?"

"Fine."

Wanda wanted to know who Rosie was, and Hal said she was a friend.

"A serious friend?"

"I've known Rosie since she was twenty-one."

"How old is she now?"

"Twenty-two."

"Hal, what plans do you have for the next ten years of your life?"

Hal sat back and studied her cute serious face under the squirrel hat. "Am I supposed to have a plan?"

"If you don't have a plan you never get anywhere."

"My plan is to get enough money to eat and pay my room rent."

"I'm serious—everybody should have some sort of plan."

"A muskrat has a plan, a moose has a plan, but a man—he does what he pleases."

She had come to the bottom of the mickey, quite fast.

"You can't just do what you please. You have to have some social responsibility. You have to do something for mankind."

Hal looked back steadily as she fastened him with her grave blue eyes. "What are you going to do for mankind, Miss Scott?"

"I'm going to be either a lawyer or a poet. Depending."

Woodrow got up. "We'd better find a table, Wanda."

"I'm having fun here."

Woodrow didn't say anything more. He threaded his way across the dance floor and left the place.

"Now you're responsible for me, Hal."

"In that case, let's dance. He lifted her to her feet and swung her out to the dance floor. She was pretty heavy on those little feet—nothing like Rosie—and his shined shoes took some dust. She complained that there was too much wax on the floor, but it wasn't the wax. She just didn't know how to dance. He steered her back to the table, and she had no trouble swallowing two more drinks, and the more she drank the more she talked. Time went on. He was thinking he ought to go and pick up Rosie and take her home when he saw Skinny Thorkelson standing against the wall. Skinny was watching them. Beside him was a fellow in a gray mackinaw and khaki pants, and he also was watching them. You could tell when somebody had an interest in you that was not for your good. This fellow had such an interest.

"I think we'd better be getting you home before your mother begins to worry."

"She won't worry. She likes me to go out and have fun. It's Dad who shivers and shakes. Thank God he's away. There's a man looking at us in a funny way, Hal."

"I know."

The fellow in the gray mackinaw crossed the dance floor, put his hand on Hal's shoulder. "Hello, Frank, how've you been?"

"His name isn't Frank," Wanda said.

"No? What is his name?"

"Hal Brady."

"Thank you, miss. I just happen to have a bench warrant for you, Mr. Brady."

Wanda's eyes popped. "You son-of-a-bitch!"

"Now, now, young ladies don't use language like that."

"You knew what his name was, you tricked me! He hasn't done anything, he's been with me all evening."

"You'll have to come with me, Mr. Brady. Transportation and sale of illicit beverages."

"I can't. I have a lady to take home. I'll come in tomorrow and straighten this out with the judge."

"You'll be in Fargo tomorrow."

"Who are you?" Wanda demanded.

"Name is Joe Stinger, young lady. I'll take you home. Come along, both of you."

Hal smiled at Wanda. "Don't worry. Good things always happen when you eat your shredded wheat—"

In the car she sat as close to Hal as she could, shrinking away from the Fed. They came around the corner and stopped in front of her house, and the fellow said he would wait till she got up the steps.

"I won't get away," Hal told him. "Let me be a gentleman and take her to the door."

They went up the steps together, the officer behind them. Wanda had her hand on the doorknob when the porch light came on and the door crashed open. Dick Scott stood in the light, tall as a silo.

"Get in the house, Wanda!" he bellowed.

Wanda backed away from him toward the end of the porch, and he went after her. Hal saw the open door as an opportunity, entered it, and passed a paralyzed Mrs. Scott on his way to the back door. It was locked, but there was no key in the lock. Mrs. Scott came after him and with remarkable speed took the key out of the cellar door, put it in the back door, and let him out. "Run!" she whispered.

He jumped off the porch, crossed the yard, and squeezed through a hedge as Scott and the Fed came around the house. By a roundabout route he worked his way to Central Avenue, got a cab, went out to the Red Lantern to pick up his car, and arrived at Toni Murphy's.

He opened the speakeasy door and saw his mistake. Joe Stinger was leaning against the bar.

Toni looked scared. "Don't fight in here, Hal. Please!"

"I never fight."

Stinger turned, the handcuffs came out of his pocket. "All right, Brady. Let's call off the games."

"Okay, okay. I'll go quietly, you don't need to use those things."

"I don't trust you."

"I don't know why you take that attitude. Toni, don't I always pay my rent? Am I a good, reliable citizen?"

George Finley came out of the men's room at the back.

"I'm in the hands of receivers, George."

"So I see. Where is the pleasure cruise heading?"

"Ask him."

"Mr. Brady is wanted in Fargo. I am taking him there."

George nodded agreeably, moved up to the bar. "Give them one for the road, Murphy. And give me one, as the principal mourner. What were you drinking, sir?"

Stinger hesitated.

"It's a cold night. You'd better have one."

Rosie came in. "Hal! Where were you? I waited and waited, you said you'd bring me home. I had to get a cab." She saw the handcuffs. "What's going on?"

"This gentleman is on his way to Fargo," George told her, "and he's taking Hal along as a traveling companion."

"It's all right, Rosie," Hal assured her, and Stinger rattled the handcuffs.

"First everybody's having a little heating fluid for the road. You'll have one?"

Rosie nodded, moved to the bar beside George.

"Mickeys all round." Toni poured generously, and Rosie handed round the drinks.

A short time later everybody was looking down at the floor, where Mr. Volstead's representative was stretched out peacefully.

"You serve a mean shot, Toni," Hal remarked.

"I didn't load it. I swear I didn't do anything." He poured himself a straight shot with a shaking hand.

"He had a few before," George observed. "Shall we all sit down and enjoy Hal's good fortune?" He led the way to a table in a corner.

"You gave him a mickey, didn't you, George?" Hal asked.

"That's what he ordered. Perhaps there was a little confusion as to what type of mickey he wanted."

Rosie had a funny look. She wasn't drinking. "Does anybody know how many mickey finns a person can take?"

Hal couldn't believe it. "You didn't give him one, Rosie?"

She looked behind her at the horizontal figure. "I'm afraid I did."

"Where did you get one? How did you happen to have it with you?"

"I generally have one with me, in case of trouble at the Prairie Dog."

George smiled. "A lady never goes out without a clean handkerchief and a mickey finn."

"He could die, you know."

"From causes unknown, Hal. Nobody here has the slightest idea what's wrong with him."

Toni leaned over the bar, whispered, "I gave him one, too."

"My God, we'd better empty him out. Let's hope it isn't too late." George got up and they carried Stinger into the back room.

Nobody knew what to give him, because it had never been necessary to induce one of Toni's customers to throw up. Hal suggested one of the green pickled eggs from the bar. Rosie thought warm water and mustard or soda.

"I don't have any in the bar. I'll call Ada, she might have some in the kitchen at home."

"That's too slow. Hal, you run down to Sullivan's."

"No, no. Raw egg whites," George insisted. "Sure-fire."

Toni had raw eggs for people who put them in beer. It was a messy job getting the egg whites between Stinger's teeth. Rosie couldn't take that and the ensuing results, and went upstairs.

"Well, we know what he had for dinner," Hal remarked when it was over.

Somebody had to stay up and watch him till he fell asleep in a more natural way, and that someone, they voted, should be Hal, since the thing had happened because of him.

It was a long three hours in the back room where

Stinger lay on a cot. Hal would have fallen asleep if he hadn't been so cold. At last the sun shone in the window to the east, brilliant through the diamonds of frost, and fell across the white face of the victim. Stinger woke up, angry and bewildered. "What are you doing here and where am I?"

"We're in Murphy's cigar store. I'm here because we saved your life. One of Toni's friends brought in a bottle of horse liniment and you nearly died, fellah. I have sat up all night by your side, giving you expert medical care."

"I bet. Where's Murphy?"

"Home in bed. Would you like hot coffee?"

The fellow began going through his pockets, in a feeble, worried way. "Where's that warrant? I had it before this happened. Where is it?"

"I don't know what warrant you mean."

"You and your friends went through my pockets!"

"Never. Absolutely. Would you arrest a man who just saved your life?"

"The way I feel right now, I'm not grateful." He closed his eyes.

Rosie came in through the hall door, shivering in her bathrobe. She looked at Stinger. "Oh, my God, he's dead!"

"No, he always looks like that. Could you make him some coffee?"

She nodded, went back upstairs, and then Toni came in, stamping his feet and blowing on his hands. "Is he alive?"

"Sure. Rosie's making coffee. He'll be all right."

Stinger was going through his pockets again, looking for the warrant. This would be a very good time to leave for Stanfield, Hal decided.

7

Hal stopped at the first place south of Larsen's farm. A girl with short yellow hair and blue eyes and adenoids came to the back door, and Hal said he was looking for Junior Larsen.

She flushed, and said Junior lived at the next place along the road.

Hal took a chance. "I'm really looking for Junior's girl." The flush deepened and went into the roots of the yellow hair, and down the plump white neck. "I'll tell you why. My car was in Larsen's yard for a couple of days, and I just have a feeling maybe Junior used it a few times to take his girl out. Do you know if he did?"

She looked behind her, but there was nobody else in the kitchen. "I don't know. I don't know anything about Junior." She came out on the step where she could see the Buick, and she looked scared.

"Anyway, his girl left something in my car and I was going to return it to her."

"Oh. What was that?"

"It's something kind of personal. I wouldn't want to tell anybody else about it."

"You can tell me. I know his girl, she's my best friend."

"You said you didn't know anything about Junior."

"I know his girl. I could take whatever it is and give it to her."

Hal said wait a minute, and he walked out to the Buick and brought back a brown paper sack and started to open it.

"No, don't!" she cried. "I don't want to see what it is."

"You don't have to see, young lady, because they're your pink panties, aren't they? You're Junior's girl."

A couple of juicy tears rolled out of the blue eyes. "Don't tell my father, please don't tell my father!"

"I won't tell your father." He held up the paper bag. "All I want to know is, Did Junior take my car over to the Stanfield bank last Friday night and hang around there with it?"

She reached for the bag, but he pulled it away. "Tell me first—did he?"

She nodded, and Hal gave her the bag. "Junior didn't rob the bank. He just took me for a ride and we parked back of the bank, and it blew up and we got out of there as fast as we could." She backed into the house and slammed the door.

On his way to the car Hal looked back. The girl was peeking out the kitchen window.

Hal went on up to Larsen's. The prairie chickens were out snipping seeds from the brush, their feathers fluffed to keep warm. A hawk went over, sailing high, making big smart-aleck arcs in the blue air.

Junior Larsen was not at home, he had gone with the team to play basketball at Anamoose. Mr. Larsen seemed less than glad to see Hal. "Did you want something?"

"Yes. You said you'd help me out, Larsen, if I needed help. They say this car was at the Stanfield bank last Friday night. You know I didn't have this car last Friday, it was here in your yard. That is, it was here unless somebody took it over to Stanfield for a little ride."

Larsen examined the button on his mackinaw cuff. The old bastard looked like a gopher ready to dive into its hole, teeth and all like a gopher. He was glad he hadn't given him two bottles of Canadian instead of one.

"Didn't you know Junior took the car over to Stanfield Friday night?"

"Junior never touched your car all the time it was here. I don't know where you got your information, but I do know one thing, you can get yourself and your car off my place right now."

"Are you afraid of something, Larsen? Are you afraid Junior robbed the bank?"

"Like hell I am. Junior is a good boy, we've never had one bit of trouble with him."

"I don't think he robbed the bank, but he was there when it was robbed. Sitting right there in my car. If you change your mind about making a statement, let me know, or let the sheriff know."

Driving back to Minot, Hal tried to think about the bank—who had robbed it, where the money was now, why Scott was so upset when his lockbox was destroyed. He thought about these things for a full ten minutes, then he returned to the springer spaniel. A damned good dog, absolutely wasted on Frenchy. Mrs. Murphy would raise Cain if he kept the dog in his room. She was very particular about dog tracks and dog hairs and stuff like that. Some old drunk could throw up in the bar, and that was just part of the business. She didn't care for dogs. Dogs made dirt. Dogs didn't make dirt, they just carried it from one human hangout to another.

When he got back, Toni Murphy had a message for him. "Wanda Scott wants you to call her. She sure is after you, Hal. You better lay off, her dad will cut you in small pieces."

"Sure, I know, Toni. I'm not going to call her back."

Toni peeked through the curtains on his front window. "What the hell is he sitting there for?"

Hal looked. A black Ford was parked across the street, its exhaust steaming. The fellow at the wheel was wearing a felt hat and a black overcoat.

"He's been there all morning. I don't like it."

"He's not a Fed."

"No, but he's a foreigner. Minneapolis license."

"I think I might know him."

"A friend?"

"Not exactly."

"It's none of my business, Hal, but do you think you might have too many things going?"

"I think I might." Hal glanced around the bar. Nobody there but one old fellow thinking his own thoughts. "Toni, have you heard anything about Boots Cunningham—any rumors about how he might have gone off the road?"

Toni hadn't. All he knew was Boots rolled over a bank and got killed. "Was there more to it?"

"Maybe. They found a bullet in the rear tire."

Toni's big brown eyes bulged. "Somebody drove him off the road? Christ! Why would anybody do that to Boots?"

Hal shrugged. "If you hear something, let me know?"

"Sure. But you be careful, Hal. It don't pay to be too curious about a thing like that."

"I'm a very careful guy, Toni." Hal grinned, went out

and got into the Buick. The black Ford didn't move as he pulled away.

He decided to go see Frenchy's dog again. A dog took your mind off things. When he drove into the yard, the springer came bouncing toward him. Frenchy didn't seem to be around. The springer trotted toward the chicken coop, stood at the door. Hal went in. Frenchy wasn't there, but he noticed a gurgling sound. He walked into the coop, saw an iron ring on the floor attached to a wooden cover about three feet across. He pulled it open, and met the face of Frenchy, looking up.

"What the hell are you doing down there?"

"Come on down and I'll show you."

Hal went down the ladder slowly, found himself in a maze of copper pipe. It was a pretty big still.

"This is quite a setup, Frenchy. Haven't the Feds smelled it yet?"

"How can you smell anything through chicken manure? You still want my dog?"

"I like that dog."

"He likes you. So take him."

"Don't give him to anybody else. I'll take him as soon as I can."

"Let's go up." Frenchy moved toward the ladder. "I don't like to stay down here very long with the lid off."

Frenchy was replacing the cover and Hal had his back to the door of the coop when the dog growled. Hal turned to see a fellow in a black overcoat coming toward him with a very unfriendly look.

"You Hal Brady?"

"Who the hell are you?" Frenchy demanded, his voice a little high. He must have thought it was a Fed.

The fellow paid no attention to him. "You got my gun and my boots. I want 'em back."

"I don't know anything about your gun and boots."

"Maybe you know something about a full load of alcohol that disappeared in front of Mae Monroe's."

Hal shook his head. "You've got the wrong man."

"You get off my place," Frenchy ordered, feeling brave once he knew it wasn't a Fed.

Usually you knew when somebody was ready to swing at you, but this guy slid out of his coat as if he was just getting ready to wash his face and hands before lunch. Hal was looking at his fancy suspenders when he received the punch on a nose that had already been broken a few times. He blinked, assembled himself for a good fight. It was not a good fight, the overcoat was out of condition. Frenchy didn't have to do anything but stand by and watch. The springer did the same.

It was over before it really got started. The man got up, brushed the chicken feathers from his front and put on his coat. "I'll get you yet, Brady. This ain't the end of it." He walked back to his car.

"What the hell was that all about?" Frenchy demanded. "I don't like you bringin' your friends out here. He saw me put the lid back on, and he probably guessed what's under the lid, and he could cause me a lot of trouble, you know that?"

"He's dumb. He won't connect anything, Frenchy."

"Just because he ain't a fighter don't mean he's dumb. What did you do to him?"

"I just borrowed his alcohol. But I never touched his gun or his boots."

"You'd better look behind you from now on."

On the way back to town Hal thought about the fellow

in the black overcoat—he was going to be a damned nuisance as long as he hung around Minot. Why didn't he go back to Minneapolis and carry on his profession?

When Hal walked into Toni's, the same old fellow was still sitting at the end of the bar, leaning over a beer.

"I see he followed you," Toni remarked.

"How did you know?"

"You forgot to wipe the blood off your upper lip."

"He thinks I took his gun and boots. All I took was his load of alcohol."

"Good fighter?"

"Hell, no. I think he's pretty dumb. I can't figure why he keeps hanging around Minot."

The old fellow with the beer spoke up. "You know who I seen him talkin' to? Dick Scott."

"See? I told you, Brady, you've got too many things going. You better look out." Toni wiped the bar with a wet gray rag. "Maybe Scott told him to beat you up."

"If he did, he isn't very good at picking his help." Hal couldn't believe the fight had been caused by anything but a personal grudge.

Rosie wasn't upstairs, she'd probably gone shopping. Rosie loved to shop.

Early in the evening he stopped at the Prairie Dog. The place had only three customers, but Rosie pretended to be very busy.

"I was out at Frenchy's and I saw his underground gin factory. Do you know where he has his still?"

"I can't talk now." Rosie trotted off.

When she came back, Hal stopped her. "Are you sore about something?"

"That girl came in here and asked me where she could find you. She hasn't got the sense of a baby robin."

"What girl?" He knew without asking.

"Wanda Scott, of course. Who else would ask a man's girlfriend where she can find him? What is this with you two anyway?"

"Nothing, Rosie. If there was something, she wouldn't have to ask you where to find me. She's just a funny school kid. I think I'm her homework."

"If you're her homework, you can't be mine too. Just think that over, friend."

"Sit down, hon. I have things to talk about. First, I've got to take that springer from Frenchy. If I don't, somebody else is going to grab him. He's a great dog."

"He's a great big dog. He needs a house, not a room." She paused and her face changed. "Maybe you should bring him in, Hal."

"I know what you're thinking—you and the dog together might get me to move. You might be right. That room isn't good enough for a good dog."

She gave him a look. "Hal, are you doing anything to get out from under the bank robbery thing?"

"I know how my car happened to be there when the bank blew up. The Larsen kid and his girl were parked behind it. Those pink panties belong to a nice little girl with yellow hair."

"Did the Larsen boy rob the bank?"

"I don't think so."

"You'd better find out who did, Hal. I don't want you going to jail."

"I'm not going to jail."

"You can't be sure."

"I'm sure. I'm not going to jail."

"You always think everything will turn out all right."

"It does, doesn't it? Rosie, do you think Dahl would rob his own bank?"

"Of course he would, if he thought he could get away with it."

"Could he use dynamite?"

"He'd be scared to death of dynamite. But he wouldn't mind hiring somebody else to blow off a finger."

Rosie got busy then, the place was filling up. Hal sat quietly, exchanging automatic hellos with people who drifted by. He went on thinking about the bank robbery. He had somehow to get it off his back, and he didn't know how he was going to do that.

He recalled Pat Kearns's story about Scott, digging furiously through the ashes and the twisted metal and the charred papers on the bank floor that Saturday morning. What was that all about? Had he kept his money in a lockbox? Why not in an account?

There was another question here, too. Most rails didn't save much, if anything. It was unlikely that a railroad bull would have enough in the bank to worry about. Suppose Scott had some other source of income, something he didn't want anybody to know about, so he kept the payments in a box. Hal couldn't imagine what other source of income Scott might have.

Violet came in with Shamrock over her arm, paused at Hal's table. "Did you know that guy from Minneapolis is still here? I think he's looking for you, Hal."

"He found me, out at Frenchy's. He's not much of a fighter."

"He might have friends, Hal. Can't you settle with him or something?"

"I don't think he'll bother me again."

Violet wasn't convinced, he could see that as she went off to sit with a couple of rails.

Hawk came in and wandered over. "You all alone, Brady? You look kind of lonesome. You want me to sit with you?"

"Thanks, Hawk, but I'm just leaving. I've got an appointment." Hal spoke to Rosie on his way out. "I'll see you later, hon."

He made a call from the cafe next door, and when he walked into the Red Pagoda, Wanda Scott was waiting in a booth. A toy waiter in a white starched coat only slightly spotted with mustard came over. Wanda ordered rye, and he went back to the bar, slapped a rye label on a pint of something and returned with it.

"Your dad won't come looking for you?" Hal asked.

"He's sleeping. He has a call for midnight, so he won't have time to track me down."

"You're afraid of him, aren't you?"

"Not enough to stay home." This time she gave him a long look from under her eyelashes.

"Maybe you shouldn't make him angry."

"He enjoys being angry and yelling and swearing. You don't, do you? You're just easy and calm, you take things as they come."

Hal said that wasn't quite true. "I love a good noisy fight. It gets your blood moving."

"I hate fights."

"You'll probably find some fighting bastard and marry him."

"Like you?" Her eyes grew soft.

"Look, Wanda, you've been calling me—what did you want?"

"'I just wanted to see you."

"Why?"

"You're the only real person I know." She put on a serious frown. There was something phony about it. "Did you rob the Stanfield bank?"

"No, did you?"

"I mean it. Some people think you did."

"They're wrong. Who put you up to asking me that, your dad?"

She flushed. So that was it. Scott was trying to find out where something had gone, probably money.

Sidney Wong, the proprietor, came in from the kitchen, greeted them politely, and asked if everything was all right. Hal said it was, and Sidney got busy changing tablecloths and wiping off sugar bowls. Hal had the impression Wong was listening, and lowered his voice.

"Why did your dad have a lockbox up there?"

"I didn't know he had." She took a long swallow from her glass. "Bob Dahl is my uncle, so of course it was natural for Dad to have an account there."

"You don't have any idea what he had in his box?"

She shook her head. "Why?"

"Somebody who saw him up there the morning after the bank was dynamited said he was pretty worked up. Down on his hands and knees pawing through the papers and stuff on the floor. Swearing."

She thought anybody who had a box in the bank would have been a little irritated.

"Sure. But this is more than a little. If it was money he lost, why was it in a box instead of a regular deposit?"

She looked down into her glass, and she didn't answer right away.

The little waiter came back with a plate of pretzels, and she ate six of them before she said anything. "Hal, you're going to think I'm not very loyal, but I'm afraid my father was in something—dangerous."

"You mean crooked?"

"I guess I mean crooked. He's been terribly nervous and irritable. Not just since the robbery. Before that. A long time before that." She stopped, folded a paper napkin into a tight little triangle. "I think he's afraid of somebody."

"Any idea who?"

She shook her head. "I shouldn't have said this to you. But you're sort of in the middle of things, you know what goes on. I thought maybe you'd heard something."

He hadn't heard anything.

"You don't think it was smuggling whiskey? On the train?"

Hal didn't think so. He'd have heard about that, being in the same line of business. "Was that bank really robbed?"

She opened up the big brown eyes. "Does anybody think it wasn't?"

Hal shrugged. "If you were running a bank and you knew it was going under, wouldn't you try to think of some handy way of saving your money?"

"Uncle Bob wouldn't do anything like that."

"Uncle Bob was president of a bank. Never mind, you'll learn these things in time. Oh, God, here comes Hawk."

"Hello, Hal. I never seen you in here before unless you was making some kind of a deal. Who's your lady friend?"

"Wanda, this is Hawk."

Hawk bent his head politely, swayed toward the table, steadied himself. "Can I buy you two a drink?"

"Thanks a lot, but we were about to leave. Say, I hear the Gopher has some real Canadian—came in tonight."

"Yeah?" Hawk looked around the Pagoda, rejected it, and after two misses, made it out the door.

"He takes pills," Hal told Wanda. "Combined with top-quality bathtub gin, they sometimes cause him to sail off the top of the stairs at the Park. He's a good guy, only he runs off at the head. I hope he doesn't see Rosie tonight."

"Is Rosie a serious girl of yours?"

"I don't have serious girls. Just funny girls."

"I liked Hawk. He's real. He's the kind of person you want to sit down and study."

Hal said the study of Hawk would require almost no sitting but a lot of running. He was always in motion.

"What I'm trying to say, Hal, is that I want to see the real people, the people who are doing things, right now, in this particular period of history. People connected with life as it is being lived. Like bootleggers and Feds."

"You know a bootlegger. Do you know any Feds?"

"No. Do you?"

Hal laughed. "They're part of my life."

"Pick out a typical one and introduce me, will you? One I can talk to."

Hal couldn't think of a Fed you could talk to. Boots came into his mind, but Boots wasn't what you'd call a Fed. And Boots was dead. A connection clicked in his mind. "Was your dad off on Sunday night?"

"That's a funny question. Why do you want to know?"

"I'm trying to make a picture out of a lot of tiny pieces."

"He was off Sunday night, he and my mother went up to Stanfield to see Uncle Bob and commiserate."

Sidney Wong brought more drinks. "On the house," he said, smiling. There was something unappetizing about the smile—Wong was nervous.

Hal asked Wanda about the young man she had been with that night in the Park Hotel.

"Woodrow? He's sure he's going blind every time he takes a sip of beer. He goes to Ohio Wesleyan and he's home this quarter because he had pneumonia and needed to rest up."

The Park Hotel, Hal said, was a very fine place to rest.

"I suppose I'll marry him. A person can't go around forever being an old maid."

"What does Woodrow talk about?"

"Whatever's in the *Atlantic Monthly*. He doesn't have thoughts, he has regurgitations of other people's thoughts. There's always something rumbling down there ready to be thrown up." She paused, looking gravely across at him through the pink lamplight. "Hal, what are your plans for the next ten years of your life?"

He was trying to think of an answer to that when the stuff hit him. He saw Wanda's frightened face, and knew he had to get out of there, fast. He pulled himself up, couldn't make it, sat down again, shaking.

Wanda was looking beyond him at someone. "It was bad liquor, he's been poisoned!"

Hal turned, saw Sidney Wong backing away. "No, no, Miss, we do not sell bad liquor here."

"I'll call our doctor."

"No." Hal made the effort again, and this time he stood, holding onto the table. "Come on." He staggered across the floor, Wanda held the door open, and he made it outside.

"Get out of the way." He threw it all up. He hated to throw up in front of anybody, especially a girl. "Can you drive?"

She could. She took him to Toni Murphy's, and Toni got him upstairs to bed.

"You should know better than to take a drink in the Pagoda. They sell anything, Hal."

Hal didn't answer. Toni was fading.

Sometime later Rosie snapped on the light, came over and sat on the bed in a quiet, friendly way. "I'm going to kill you, Hal."

"Wait a couple of hours and you might not have to."

"Toni called me. He said you were pretty sick. I grabbed my coat, but on the way out of the Prairie Dog I met Hawk."

Hal waited.

"Hawk saw you in the Pagoda with Wanda Scott."

"Hawk talks too much. He's a regular old woman."

"You didn't say he was lying." She was angry, and she was crying.

"Rosie!" He put his arms around her. "Don't cry. It was strictly business with Wanda and me. I wanted to find out if there was a link between Scott and the Stanfield bank."

"You knew there was a connection. I told you Mrs. Scott was Dahl's sister."

Hal said it had occurred to him that Scott had some special reason for keeping his cash secret. He wanted to ask Wanda about it.

"You could have asked her about that in front of the bakery in the middle of the afternoon, you didn't have to take her into that dark Pagoda and buy her a lot of drinks and—"

"And what? Rosie, I threw up all over the place. I was in no shape for making love. Know what I think?"

"I don't even care what you think. I'm taking my velvet chair and I'm leaving, the first thing in the morning."

"Why don't you leave now?"

"I'm too tired."

8

Hal woke to find Rosie up and dressed. She was bending over her old steamer trunk.

"What time is it?"

"Nine o'clock."

"What are you doing up in the middle of the night?"

"I told you last night I'm leaving." She slammed the lid and locked it.

"Come on, Rosie, don't be mad. That funny kid doesn't mean anything to me. You know what she asked me: 'Mr. Brady, what are your plans for the next ten years of your life?'"

Rosie looked at him quietly as she put on her coat, buttoned it, and picked up her handbag. "Hawk is coming for my trunk and my chair."

Hal was beginning to see she meant it. "You'd better think this over, Rosie."

"I've thought it over. I'm leaving."

"Damn it, I'll help you." He got up, opened the window, lifted the trunk and heaved it over the sill. It made quite a bang, hitting the sidewalk, but it didn't break. It was a well-made trunk.

Rosie slammed the door and went click-click-click

down the stairs. She would be back, he told himself. She always forgot something.

He told George about it, over breakfast in Sullivan's. "Where do you suppose she went?"

"I don't know. She's pretty sore at you, Hal. And maybe with some reason."

"Reason, hell. Wanda doesn't mean a thing to me! She kept calling me, and I kept not calling her back, and then I thought maybe I could find out something from her about her father's lockbox in the Stanfield bank."

"Did you?"

"No. She wanted to find out something from *me*. She asked me if I robbed the bank, and I think Scott put her up to that. He wants to know who got his money. She told me she suspected he was in something crooked, but maybe that was just a come-on to see if I knew what games he was playing. Then I got that no-good drink."

"A very interesting evening," George decided.

"I can't figure it out. Why would somebody try to knock me out or kill me with bad liquor at the Pagoda?"

George stirred his coffee. "I don't know. Maybe it was just bad liquor by accident, Hal. It happens in the best places."

"I don't think so. I've had bad liquor before, and this didn't taste like Grandma's favorite recipe. There was a kind of chemical taste—metallic—and Sidney Wong was standing behind me waiting for me to fall over."

"Was Wanda sick?"

"Not a bit."

George wondered if Scott and Sidney Wong might be tied up in the same business.

"But what is the business?"

"Something sufficiently criminal to make them very nervous. They're afraid you are getting too close to it."

Hal didn't see how he could be so close to something and not know what it was.

"You've got to find out what it is and who they are before they kill you, Hal."

Hortense came over, looking pleased. "I hear Rosie left you, serves you right. No nice girl would live over that rotten speakeasy."

"Who said I cared about losing her? Do you know where she went?"

Hortense didn't know. "Are you busy today, Hal?"

"What did you have in mind?"

"I thought if you weren't busy you could paint the bathroom in the flat."

Hal didn't say no right away, and that was a mistake. You had to have all your loose ends tucked in or Hortense would grab you by one of them. She didn't even say she'd buy the paint.

Hawk came in, and Hal asked him where Rosie was.

"Geez, I don't know, Hal. Honest I don't know."

"She said you were picking up her trunk and her chair."

"Her chair? Geez, I forgot the chair."

"Where did you take the trunk?"

"I can't tell you, she told me not to tell you."

"Never mind. I don't care where she went."

Hawk looked relieved, sat down and had a plate of fried oysters, his usual breakfast. He said the Boosters were in town, and ready to work orders if they had any. Hal thought maybe they could get the paint for Barney's bathroom.

Violet appeared, with Shamrock on her arm, and Hawk, who liked her pretty well, asked her to sit down.

Violet said Mae Monroe was thinking over George's idea about sewing machines for the girls. "She hates to put out the money, though."

Hawk told her the Boosters could get the machines.

"The Boosters?" Violet repeated.

George was surprised she didn't know who they were. "They transfer merchandise from a store to an eager customer without the nuisance of a clerk writing up a ticket."

"You mean they steal things?"

"Some people might call it that. Actually, they are promoting the rapid movement of consumer goods. They aid commerce."

"They steal things, and you buy from them?"

"At a considerable discount."

Violet smiled. "Mae does like a discount."

"Say, Hal," Hawk said, "are you sure it's all right if I come to the wedding? I always liked old Barney, I want to say goodbye."

"Goodbye?"

"Hortense is goodbye, ain't she?"

Hal looked hard into Hawk's big blue marble eyes. "Where did you take Rosie's trunk?"

"I can't tell you, Hal. I'd like to, but Rosie said she'd kill me if I told you. I wonder what I should get Barney for a wedding present?"

"An alarm clock. They have so many jobs they'll need one." Hal turned to George. "Why don't we paint their bathroom? That would be a nice wedding present."

George said no thanks, but presently the two of them went over to measure the bathroom and see how much paint it would take. Hortense had rented this flat over a shoe-repair shop in an old building near Sullivan's so she and Barney could walk to work. They couldn't afford a car. When Hal and George unlocked the place it smelled like old shoes. There were cracks in the plaster, and the front room was a blue that set your teeth on edge.

"Let's paint the whole thing," Hal suggested.

"A man whom someone is trying to murder, and whose girl has just disappeared, has nothing better to do than paint this hopeless dwelling."

Hal said he could think while painting, and right now they had to order some paint. They found a Booster named Clarence who delivered two gallons of paint to the flat in less than an hour.

"I hope you like the colors," he said. "They was the handiest to the door." One can was lavender and one was lettuce green.

"Why didn't you at least get two of the same color?" George demanded.

"At this price, you gotta take what comes. You don't know how hard it is to get out with a gallon. Quarts is easy. Next time you order quarts."

"I'm ordering quarts right now," Hal decided. "Get me eight quarts of any color white."

Clarence said he couldn't go back to the same lumber yard, too risky.

"There's a couple more on the other side of town. Go work them. And get brushes too."

Clarence left, and they took the rusty screen off the front-room window. "You might be making a mistake, Hal," George warned. "You should always ask a woman what she wants before you give it to her."

"She'll be tickled to death to have a nice fresh paint job in here. Anybody would."

George lifted an eyebrow but he didn't say any more.

Clarence came back. "I got some off-white and some on-white, and the quarts wasn't easy, they was on a shelf behind the counter, but I got a friend to go in with me and buy two bits' worth of chicken wire and they had to go out back and cut that. So I have to add the two bits' to the price."

"You'd think one lumber yard would warn another about what's going on," George observed.

"You don't understand the lumber business," Hal told him. "Old man Crane loses two gallons of paint, he wants Nepfer to lose three gallons."

Clarence collected for the paint, then he said he understood there was to be a wedding and did anybody need a new suit. Hal counted his money, and considered.

"You'll look good—the girls will go for you," Clarence urged. "Maybe because you look good, something will come your way that you don't expect."

"Like a spell in jail. What do you say, George? Shall we go for a new suit?"

George was for it.

"You want to make a down payment?"

"No," Hal said. "You'll get your money when I get the suit."

"Okay. I didn't think you would."

George was not a very good painter, and this worried Hal. "Get the corners," he pleaded. "And don't try to do any windows, you smear it all over the panes."

"For a guy who can sleep in a boxcar and cook in a tin can under a bridge, you're plenty fussy."

"That's different. That's from necessity. When you do a job of work you want to do it right."

George didn't think Hortense would notice—anyway, not till the honeymoon was over.

"I wonder why I'm doing this for her."

"So do I."

It was a slow job. Hal insisted on patching the cracks and doing it right. George grumbled and said they ought to be looking for Rosie.

"She'll show up tonight at the Prairie Dog."

"I hope you're right."

Rosie did not appear at the Dog, nor did she call Homer to say why she wouldn't be there. At least that was what Homer told Hal and George.

"I think he knows where she is," Hal said. "She's sore and she told him not to let me know."

The next morning they went back to the flat and continued painting. Around noon, Clarence the Booster came up. "I ran into trouble, boys. Word is getting around town and the clerks is on to us, a fellow don't have half a chance. I'm sorry about the suits, but I can't fill the order. We're clearing out of Minot."

"That's all right," Hal told him. "We don't really need new suits anyway. Did you get any sewing machines for Mae Monroe?"

"Yeah, we got one. A dandy. It was more of a job to get the money out of that old girl than it was to get the machine out of the store."

They went on painting and by late afternoon had almost finished the job. Hortense came in, carrying a bunch of coat hangers and a can of chicken soup. She stopped short.

"My God. You painted it white!"

"Isn't it nice?" George asked. "Your brother-in-law is a very careful painter. He even fills the cracks."

"White," she repeated, swinging her eagle nose around the room.

"You don't like it."

"I liked the color it was."

The hair on Hal's neck prickled. "That's too bad, Hortense. We'll scrape it down to that beautiful throw-up blue."

"It was nice of you to think of it, Hal. I don't mean to

be ungrateful, only white isn't for a front room, it's for bathrooms. Say, could you get the chairs at Packer's funeral parlor? And Barney wants you to pick up his suit at Nickie's tomorrow morning because he won't get off work at Hayden's till six o'clock and Nickie will be closed." Her eyes traveled over the room, as sharp as a piecework foreman's. "You didn't paint the back of that door. Have you heard from Rosie?"

Hal said he hadn't.

"Aren't you worried? She's fed up with you, Hal, and I don't blame her. Do you, George?"

George pretended not to hear, and Hortense left.

"We'll quit now, and I'll come back tonight and paint that damned door," Hal decided. He was anxious to get over to the Prairie Dog. All day he had counted on finding Rosie there at her usual time maybe not ready to forgive him, but softening up a little.

Rosie was not at the Prairie Dog.

"Rosie never let me down like this," Homer complained. "If she couldn't come she always called up, and generally she got another girl to take her place."

"You mean you don't know where she is?"

"No, I don't."

"I thought everybody was keeping it from me because she told them to. She was plenty sore when she left."

"She's probably sore, Hal. Maybe she went up to her sister's in Stanfield."

"I called her sister. She doesn't know where Rosie is—anyway, she said she didn't. She might be lying. I don't rate too high with Mary."

"Call her again," George suggested.

Hal went into the back room and called Stanfield. This

time he knew Mary wasn't lying. He tried to be reassuring. "Rosie's just having a good time making me worry."

"But why would she want to worry me?" Mary demanded.

"She didn't think of that. She'll be at Barney's wedding Sunday, you can be sure of that."

"I wish I could be."

"I think you'd better tell the police," Homer suggested.

"Hell of a lot they'd help. If she's been kidnaped they're probably in on it." All the same, Hal went down to the station and gave the story to a fat old cop who listened as if it was a complaint about thistles in a vacant lot.

On the way out he met Squeaky and told him about Rosie, thinking it would make more of an impression on Squeaky, who knew her. It did. "Jesus, Hal, you think somebody's kidnaped her?"

"I don't know. If you hear anything, let me know right away, will you?" Hal gave him a couple of bills, and Squeaky gave his earnest promise.

His mind was now going in several directions at once—Did Rosie's disappearance have something to do with the thing Dick Scott was in? He had no faith at all in the ability of the local police to find Rosie. Maybe it would help to get Gordon McGee in on this—a sheriff could cover more territory, and McGee had a sharper mind. At the same time, Hal kept hoping that Rosie would just walk into the Dog as if nothing had happened. He went back to see. She wasn't there.

He put in his second call to Stanfield that night, and it occurred to him that Rosie would consider all this telephoning pretty extravagant. He got McGee at home.

"I'm sorry, Brady, but I can't mess around in that county. They'd be sore as hell—out of my jurisdiction. But I'll see if I can find out something without stepping on toes. You sure your girl isn't just punishing you a little— What I hear, you're a pretty casual fellow."

"Could be," Hal admitted. "By the way, have you found the guy that wrecked Boots's car?"

"No. Not even a lead. What's your special interest in that, Brady? You suspect anything or anybody?"

"No, nobody. I'm just puzzled. There was a guy everybody liked, never did anybody any harm."

McGee agreed it was strange, but he thought clues would turn up in the course of time.

Hal hung up, reflecting that everybody seemed willing to let nature take its course, nobody was giving nature any help. Well, there wasn't anything more he could do tonight—he might as well go paint Hortense's door. He had a couple of drinks first.

It was a dark night, no moon, and the small lot behind the Dog was full of dimly outlined cars, but Hal spotted a familiar black Ford. It was parked at the other side, and as he got into the Buick he could see a fellow behind the wheel, but he wasn't sure it was the third-rate fighter in the black overcoat.

He drove over to the building, climbed the wooden stairs. There was an odor, but he didn't identify it. He lit a cigarette and opened the door of Barney's flat.

When he came to he was lying at the bottom of the stairs and George was bending over him.

"Well, Brady, what are your plans for the next ten years?"

Somebody outside was yelling, "Get him out of there before the whole damn building goes up!"

George dragged him outside and a couple of fellows

picked him up and dumped him in a car. George was at the wheel, and he bulled his way through hoses and firemen.

"Where are you going?" Hal demanded, sitting up.

"Hospital."

"What for? I don't need a hospital."

"You must have gone down those stairs like a bullet."

"I'm all right." Hal felt his legs and his head. "Nothing's broken."

"Who knew you were going back up there, Hal? How many people did you talk to in the Dog?"

"Just Homer. You think somebody turned on the gas in the flat?"

"Yes. Somebody rather unfriendly."

"But nobody knew when I was going back. I didn't know myself exactly when."

"They didn't need to know exactly when, as long as they knew it would be sometime during the evening. They just went up there and turned on the gas."

"The door was locked—but any old passkey would have opened it. I'm haunted by that fellow from Minneapolis. When I came out of the Dog he was parked in the lot, sitting in his car."

"Did he follow you?"

Hal didn't know. "But if he wants to kill me, George, he could have done it a dozen times. He acts like a dog chasing a rabbit and afraid to catch it. Do you think he's still sore about the boots and the gun that he thinks I stole? Sore enough to kill me?"

George shook his head. "Somebody else hired him to kill you or incapacitate you."

"If they did, they're not very good at selecting skilled labor. He's about as clumsy as the guy that blew up the Stanfield bank. Nobody would hire him."

"Why not? You think everybody else knows what they're doing. You think if somebody hires a killer he picks one who is smart, efficient and experienced. Maybe such a perfect killer is not available at the moment. Maybe this person who has taken a dislike to you hasn't had much experience in choosing killers."

"But why does he want me dead?"

"Why would somebody want Boots Cunningham dead?"

At the hospital a fellow in a white coat gave Hal a few minutes, about the time allowed for dipping a sheep, and said he was okay, but if anything went wrong during the night to come back.

George helped him up the stairs to his room. "Want me to stay, just in case?"

"No, I'm all right." Hal stretched out on the unmade bed.

"What really makes me mad is all that work we put in painting the flat, George. All wasted."

"You've got to find out who it is, Hal. Stop horsing around painting other people's privies and pay some attention to what's going on. Maybe they've got Rosie."

"My God, George." Hal sat up. "You mean that?"

"I mean it. Get some sleep, and in the morning you'd better start looking for her."

Hal listened to George's footsteps fading down the stairs, and wished Rosie was there with him. Rosie or Frenchy's springer spaniel. Rosie wouldn't like being bracketed with a dog, even a good dog. His eye fell on her blue velvet chair. Funny she hadn't sent for that, if she was all right.

Between listening for hostile noises, and worrying about Rosie, he spent a bad night.

9

Early in the morning, Barney came in, all worry and frown. "What happened?"

"I'm all right, kid. Perfectly all right."

"George says you were blown down the stairs. You could have been killed."

"But I wasn't. I just feel sorry for you kids losing your flat. Maybe Hortense will postpone the wedding."

"She'll find another flat." Barney went off to work, and Hal slowly made his way to Sullivan's.

Hortense was coming out with her coat on.

"I could kill you, Hal Brady. First you get Barney in jail, then you blow up our flat. You'll do anything to stop this wedding, won't you?"

"My God, Hortense, I didn't blow up the flat."

"Who did, then? You were the one they found at the bottom of the stairs, nobody else was there, and you and George were in there painting so you left the gas on, having coffee."

"We never turned on anything. All we did was paint."

It was no use telling Hortense somebody was trying to kill him. She didn't readily accept fantastic ideas.

"I got the flat over Hayden's store," she told him.

"Thank God we didn't have our furniture moved in yet. You're going to pick up Barney's suit right away, aren't you? Nickie closes at one. And then get the funeral chairs. I'll see you later at the house."

"Mind if I eat my breakfast first?"

Nickie had the suit ready, and it was a beautiful job. Barney would be pleased. Maybe even Hortense would be pleased.

"You look good, you feel good," Nickie told them. "A man thinks he's a millionaire, pretty soon he gets to be a millionaire."

"How come you never did, Nickie?"

"I got no time for such foolishness. I got to work."

Hal bought a new tie and took Barney's suit up to the room, laid it carefully on the blue velvet chair. Next he drove over to the funeral parlor for the chairs. When he got to the house, Hortense and her mother and a gang of women were making little sandwiches with no crusts and wrapping them in damp dishtowels. Mrs. Beiermeister, a meek, sad little woman with a twist of gray hair and a thin wrinkled neck, was no match for Hortense, nor for old man Beiermeister either. He was sitting on the back porch spitting tobacco juice and muttering at the chickens.

"No lunch, house full of cackling females. Don't spit, Gus, don't track in mud, Gus, don't breathe, Gus. A man can't call his soul his own."

"Never mind," Hal told him, "it'll all be over tomorrow."

"No, it won't. We'll be eatin' them goddam lettuce sandwiches for a month. Why didn't she just go get married? They still got justices of the peace in this town.

Why did she have to make my life hell for two weeks just to get that bastard brother of yours?"

Hal carried chairs into the house until Hortense was satisfied no more could be squeezed in.

"Did you get Barney's suit?" she asked.

"I did."

"I hope you put it on a hanger." She paused, reading a list. "Now you can go get the plates and cups."

"Why don't you use paper plates?"

"Paper plates! For my wedding?" Hortense glared. "And pick up the punch bowl, too, Hal. At Edith's."

"You having punch?"

"Of course. But no liquor. And if you or any of your crazy friends pour anything into it, you'll be sorry."

"A man needs something to cheer him up at his wedding."

When he came back with the punch bowl, she said, "You can bring Wanda Scott if you want to."

"Wanda! What for?"

"I just thought you might want to bring her. You been taking her out, haven't you?"

"Hortense, where the hell is Rosie?"

"Rosie? I don't know."

He got away before Hortense could think of any more little jobs for him. On his way around town he invited several friends to the wedding. All the time he was doing this, he was also thinking about Rosie. Whenever he met someone who knew her, he asked where she was hiding out. Nobody would tell him. He cruised the familiar streets, but there wasn't a girl who looked like Rosie walking on any of them.

At six o'clock he and George drove over to Hayden's to

pick up Barney and take him around on his last night of freedom. Mr. Hayden had let him off early and he had already left.

"We'll go get him," Hal said. "Maybe we can make him change his mind about the whole thing."

"You can't do that, Hal. Think of all those lettuce sandwiches going to waste."

They found Barney at Beiermeister's, wiping up the kitchen floor, and they got him in a corner and said this was it, he'd done his duty for the day, and they were taking him out. Barney looked at Hortense, flinging a skillet on the stove to fry some tough meat for supper.

Hal took him by one arm and George the other, and they got him out the front door and into the Buick. Hortense ran after them. "Don't you get him drunk, Hal Brady!"

"Sure, get him drunk, Hal," her father called.

They decided Barney would have a better time in his new suit, so they stopped by Hal's and made him put it on.

"If anything happens to this suit, I might as well shoot myself," Barney warned.

"What could happen to it?" Hal demanded. "We're taking you to one of the best speakeasies in town."

They started at the Park Hotel, went on to the Gopher and a new place where the liquor tasted like the stuff O'Connor made, hairy and leafy, and somewhere they had tamales and coffee, and then started over. Barney didn't look too well when they decided about four o'clock to call it a night, so Hal took him up to his own room, got him out of his clothes, and let him down gently on the bed. Something wasn't right, but while Hal was trying to think what it was, he fell asleep.

Don't Wake Me Up While I'm Driving

He woke with a start. Sunlight lay across the bed and the ceiling was going by slowly. He knew what was wrong. The blue chair was gone. So Rosie wasn't kidnaped. She'd come for her chair! She might still be sore at him, but at least she was in Minot, alive and circulating.

He woke Barney. "If you want to get married, get up. If you don't, go back to sleep."

Barney looked pretty bad, but he seemed to feel he ought to go to his own wedding. It wasn't until he put on the new coat that they discovered one sleeve was all but ripped out of the armhole.

"When did I do that?" he wondered. "Hortense will kill me."

"I was in a fight with somebody, but I didn't think you were anywhere near, Barney." Hal examined the damage. It was only the thread that was torn. Nickie could sew in the sleeve.

George came along, and the three of them drove over to Nickie's. He wasn't there, he had gone to Anamoose for a family celebration. They drove through the empty streets, looking for tailors. Minot on a Sunday morning was deserted except for an occasional clutch of little girls in hair ribbons on their way to Sunday school, and an odd drunk or two leaning in a doorway to throw up. They found two tailors, neither of whom would do the job. George thought there must be a girl, among all the girls they knew, who had a machine and knew how to use it. What about the girls in Mae Monroe's House? The Boosters had delivered one machine to Mae.

They drove up to the Hill, rang the bell. It took some time for Mae to answer it. She looked tired, and said the night before had been rough, and what did they want at this hour? They followed her into the parlor and showed her Barney's suit. "We have to get it together again before the wedding at two o'clock. Somebody said you got a machine from the Boosters, Mae."

"I got one, yes. Hell of a lot of good it does me. Nobody knows how to make it run. I bought all this stuff to sew. I'm out fifteen dollars and twenty-seven cents. And I don't think the cops are going to go for the idea my girls are earning a living on piecework." She waved a flabby arm at several piles of pink and blue material lying on a red plush sofa. George picked up a sample baby bonnet.

Violet appeared and was very sympathetic, but she couldn't sew.

"Go see if anybody here can sew on a machine," Hal ordered. "I'll hook it up and get it running."

Barney sat on a straight chair, looking sick.

Hal attached the cord to an outlet and then he and George tried to thread the thing. There was no manual—the Boosters had overlooked the manual. Hal pressed the foot pedal and the machine took off.

"Give me something to sew on."

George handed him a baby bonnet and Hal was stitching the bonnet when Squeaky Simpson walked in. It took Squeaky some time to realize that he was seeing what he was seeing.

"I didn't know you could sew, Brady. What is it you're makin'?"

"What do you mean, Simpson, coming in here without ringing the bell?" Mae demanded.

"I just came to collect, ma'am. I got to carry out my orders. But I never thought I'd see the day Hal Brady would be sittin' here in the parlor, sewin' baby bonnets." He sank into a soft chair, chuckling. "I got to call the station so everybody can come up here. They'll never believe it if I tell 'em."

Violet came back with one of the girls. "Nadine can sew," she said.

"I made a pair of basketball bloomers in 4-H Club. That's the only thing I ever made. But I'll try."

Barney looked on without interest. Violet offered him chocolate-covered cherries from a big pink box, and he had to go outside. When he reappeared, slightly greener, they made him put on the jacket.

"It's a co-operative masterpiece, like the League of Nations," George said. "Of course that fell apart."

Squeaky, having accepted a roll of bills from Mae Monroe, started toward the door. Hal stopped him. "Have you heard anything about Rosie?"

Simpson gave him a shifty smile. "Nothing, Hal. Honest, I ain't heard a thing about Rosie. Not a thing." The shifty smile was normal, but the protest was too strong.

"You know something, don't you?"

"No, Brady, I don't know a damned thing. Not one damned thing." Squeaky hurried away.

Hal always felt like taking a bath after a conversation with Simpson. "I think he's heard something. I'm going down to the station."

"You can't!" Barney cried. "It's too late. Wait till after the wedding."

"He looked as if he was lying."

"He always looks as if he's lying," George muttered. "Come on. We'll check him out later."

Hortense was in a lather. She had gotten into her wedding dress, a tight lacy thing halfway between Mae West and Lady Diana Manners, but she had a lot of trotting to do yet, so she was still wearing her sneakers, and her hair was wound on toilet paper. Mrs. Beiermeister was washing glasses. The old man sat on the only comfortable chair in the front room, a tin can on his lap so he wouldn't have to go out to spit.

"You're late, Barney," the bride snapped. "Let's see your suit. Don't tell me Nickie put that sleeve in like that. It's gathered!"

They told her what had happened. She didn't seem to think it was inconsiderate of Barney to get into a fight in his new suit—what outraged Hortense was that they had mended it in a whorehouse. "Don't you know you catch things in a place like that?"

"What things, Hortense?" Hal teased.

"Crabs, for one thing. Barney, what's the matter with you? You look sick. Where did you take him last night, Hal? You got him drunk, didn't you?"

Hal said that was the custom, a man was supposed to get soused the night before his wedding.

"It's a rotten custom."

"You wouldn't want him to get soused the night after?"

Hortense ran the carpet sweeper around her father, gave it to Barney to put away, and then began shoving things around on the crocheted tablecloth—spoons and forks, paper napkins, somebody's glass candlesticks, somebody else's hand-painted china plate piled with sandwiches. She went to the kitchen and came back with a glass bowl of pink and white carnations. Hal saw with some surprise that Hortense's hands were shaking as she set the bowl on the table.

"Come on, kid," he said, "it isn't that serious. Don't be scared."

"Who said I was scared?"

Sullivan arrived with the cake, which he himself had made. "How goes it?" he asked. "You ask me, I feel sorry for both of them."

"I know," George agreed. "I have days when I feel sorry for all mankind, but this passes if I have a good lunch."

"Is Rosie here, Hal?"

"No."

"I was sure she'd turn up at the wedding." Sullivan looked troubled.

"So was I."

"She might turn up yet. She's still got time."

The preacher's car pulled into the yard and Hortense skinned out of sight to comb her hair and put on her satin pumps. The preacher came in with his wife. "I'm Marvin Grimsrud, and this is Mrs. Grimsrud." He shook hands with everybody and did not disguise his interest in Hal Brady, that notorious bootlegger. He tried to engage Barney in conversation, but Barney was unable to respond, his mind riveted to the ordeal ahead of him—saying the right words and not making a fool of himself. George came to their rescue, George could talk to anybody.

Hortense came out of the bedroom looking almost pretty, her small eyes bright, her long thin face flushed under the powder. The small house was filling up, and the overflow spilled onto the glassed-in front porch. When it looked as if you couldn't crowd in another pair of Sunday shoes, Hortense found her voice.

"We better start! Where's Barney?"

"I'm here, Hortense."

"Dad, wipe your mouth and get ready to give me away."

They all took their places, and Hal was thinking somebody ought to be giving Barney away, but he wouldn't want to be the one to do it. The preacher took the opportunity to lecture a larger audience than he'd had in church that morning on the sanctity of marriage, the way to bring up children, the evils of drink—with his eye on Hal—and other items of morality. Finally he reached the meat of the business, Barney squeezed the ring on Hortense's finger, and was about to kiss her when two cars bounced into the yard, dumped out seven or eight familiar characters, each carrying a bottle. Hawk led them to the porch, and the old man, recognizing not only friends, but friends with refreshment, opened the door.

"Don't let them in, they'll spoil everything!" Hortense cried. But they were already in. They gathered round the punch bowl, where there was a steady gurgling sound, and then they carried the empty bottles to the kitchen. Hawk, holding a cup of punch in his big hairy hand, began to look around. They had brought their own mood into the house, but now they began to feel the presence of the preacher and his wife, they noticed the scrubbed ears, the shined shoes of various men of their acquaintance and the way Hortense was watching them as she tried to say polite sentences to a couple of plump females in tight corsets. Barney was not watching anybody—after a piece of wedding cake his stomach was engaging his whole attention. He leaned against the wall near the front door, thinking he might have to make a dash for it.

"You hear about Frenchy?" Hawk asked. "The Feds picked him up."

"My God," Sullivan said. "Poor Frenchy."

"Who has his dog?" Hal demanded. Nobody knew.

Hawk poured another bottle into the punch. "Say, Hal, I hope you didn't care if I went up to your room when you wasn't there and got Rosie's chair for her."

"Where is she?"

"I don't know."

"You must know if she told you to get the chair. You had to see her."

"No, Hal. The morning I picked up her and her trunk I was supposed to go back and get the chair and leave it with Mabel Carey, but I forgot until yesterday."

Hal looked at Hawkspeare and knew he was telling the truth. Hawk was no good at lying. "Does Mabel Carey know where she is?"

"I don't think so, she didn't even know about the chair, but I left it with her anyway."

"Hawk, you've got to tell me where you took Rosie when you picked her up with her trunk. Nobody knows where she is."

"Sure, Hal. You got a right to know, even if she did tell me not to say. I took her to the bus station."

"Where did she say she was going?"

"She didn't say." Hawk had a kindly, anxious frown as he put a hand on Hal's shoulder. "She's bound to come back soon, Hal. Rosie ain't the kind of girl to stay mad."

"I hope you're right. I hope she's just sore at me, and nothing has happened to her."

"Nothin's gonna happen to Rosie. She knows her way around."

Old man Beiermeister washed down a handful of mint pillows with a swallow of coffee. "I hear they found another dead Chinaman on the Soo. Funny how they keep turnin' up."

"They get in them warm compartments at the end of a fruit car, and the fumes from the stoves kills 'em off," Hawk informed him. "But how the hell do they get on the train to start with? Somebody lettin' 'em through at the line? So much a head?"

"How awful." Mrs. Grimsrud shuddered. "They just suffocate?"

"They don't feel nothin'," Beiermeister told her. "Chinamen don't feel a thing."

She gave him a look. "They are human, you know."

"Takes a woman to say that about a Chink."

She got her coat from the bedroom and she and her husband left.

Hortense watched them go without a word. Then she began to cry.

Barney put an arm around her. "Never mind, Hortense. He did his part, you're Mrs. Barney Brady now, and we'll have a better time without him."

Sullivan came over with a water glass full of punch. "Here, kid, drink this and you won't give a damn who goes home."

She seemed about to knock the glass from his hand, then she snatched it and drank the whole thing. Barney watched her, unbelieving.

"That's the girl," Sullivan cried and gave her a refill, half from the punch bowl and half from a flask in his hip pocket. After that, Hortense had the look of a hawk sailing very high above a cornfield. Everybody else wanted another drink, and a car went after more gin. It was becoming a pretty good party.

Barney was smiling, a tin cup in his hand. "I feel better, for some reason. Have you seen Hortense lately?"

"No. She's probably out under the table."

Barney soberly lifted a corner of the crocheted cloth. "No, Hal, she's not." He cruised to her bedroom off the kitchen, came back to report she was not there.

One of the girls said Hortense had gone to the outhouse.

"Maybe she passed out," Hawk suggested, taking another sip. "Somebody better go look."

At that moment Hortense came through the front door. "There's a bomb in the outhouse! It's ticking! It's ready to go off! Don't anybody go out there. Call the police!"

"Nobody's calling the law around here," her father growled.

Hal and Barney and George made their way along the path between the buckbrush and last summer's dead grass. George turned around. "Do you think she's off her rocker, too much strain getting this thing together?"

Too much punch bowl, more likely, Hal thought.

Barney said it could be a bomb. "That old man of hers would think a bomb was a big joke."

They paused at the door of the privy. Something was ticking.

Hawk came along, looking sheepish. "It ain't no bomb, Hal. It's a wedding present. I got them an alarm clock, like you said, and I wound it before I come. I had to go right after we got here, and I brought it with me, and the damn thing fell off the seat into the other hole."

They started back to the house, but Hawk stopped them. "Hortense thinks it's a bomb, she's going to be disappointed. A bride should have what she expects on her wedding day. I just happen to have a couple of sticks of dynamite in the truck—"

"No, Hawk," George told him. "It's a kind and generous offer, but the neighbors might be envious. Old man Beiermeister gets his outhouse blown up, they'll all want their outhouses blown up."

All in all, it was quite a wedding, and some people had

a good time at it, which was about all you could expect from any wedding, Hal reflected. But he had expected something else. He had been certain Rosie would be there. George went off with Hawk and his friends, and Hal got into the Buick. He didn't feel like going on with this celebration. So Rosie had left town, gone off on the bus with her trunk. Well, wait till she found out how hard it was to get a job in Spokane or Seattle or wherever she was. Wait till she began to think of all her friends here, and her sister Mary and the little girls. She'd come back.

He was driving out of the yard when Squeaky Simpson drove in, shouted at him. "Wait, Brady, I got to see you." He came over and leaned in the window. "You want to make a little money?"

"I'm not breaking into any more banks."

"No, no. This is legitimate. A friend of mine is desperate for a bartender just for a few days. He'll pay ten dollars a day, Brady."

That was about double what bartenders were getting. "Which bar?"

Squeaky looked down at his knees, squirmed a little. "It's in Whitney. Montana."

"That's quite a way to go even for ten dollars a day."

"He'll buy your gas. He's anxious."

"Seems like he could find somebody a little closer. What's wrong with this bar?"

"Nothing, Hal. It's a beautiful bar. Quiet little town where a man could do some serious thinking about his future."

Hal sat there, still looking at Squeaky. There was something a little fishy about this deal.

"Sure was too bad about Frenchy, wasn't it?"

"Yes. Damned shame."

"I was wondering if anybody took his dog. That's a good hunting dog. I could use him myself."

"Like hell you will. Frenchy gave me that dog and I'm going out to get him right now."

"Okay, okay. I didn't know that. I just didn't want the dog to go hungry." Squeaky continued to lean in the window. "That's a good job in Whitney, Hal. I'd like to see you take it. Give you a break."

He had known Squeaky most of his life, and never before had Squeaky wanted to give him a break. "What's the name of this bar?"

"I don't know if it has a name. It's the only one there."

"I may go. I'll see, after I get the springer."

10

When Hal drove into Frenchy's yard the springer came bouncing toward him, wagging and barking. "Well, fellah, did they run off and leave you?" He opened the car door. "Come on, you're my dog now. Or I'm your man, we'll see which."

The springer kept on wagging, but he wouldn't jump in. Instead, he ran toward the chicken coop, stopped to see if Hal was following, came back to get him.

"He's not down there any more, you might as well come with me."

The dog made another try, whining. Hal took him by the collar, led him to the car, and he got in. He had a handsome, commanding look, sitting on the front seat. He would have done very well in a Pierce Arrow. "Your name is Fred now. You're joining a man with quite a few pressing problems. First, I've lost my girl. Second, I think somebody is trying to kill me. Third, when my landlady sees you she is going to raise the rent." Hal made up his mind, gathered a couple of suits of underwear, four pairs of socks, and they were on their way. As they passed Sullivan's, George was coming out. Hal pulled over to the curb.

"I'm going up to Whitney and take a bartending job for a few days."

"What shall I tell Rosie if I see her?"

"You won't see her. She's left the country." He paused. "You want to come along for the ride?"

"No thanks."

Hal was glad George had said no. He wanted to go alone.

Driving along the frozen ruts out on the open prairie he had a feeling of freedom, of letting go. Fred sat forward with his paws on the edge of the seat and took note of every rabbit, every gopher, every hawk, his stub tail going, his whiskers alive. It was almost too cold to pee, but Hal stopped. One good thing about hard times, a man could stop and take care of things anywhere along the way and nobody would see him, there were only two or three cars on the road all day.

He was coming into Williston when he brought out a thought that had been at the bottom of his mind all day. Maybe he shouldn't have left Minot just now. Maybe somebody would need him. Maybe something nobody expected was waiting around a dark corner.

What the hell is the matter with you, Brady? Nothing new is going to happen in Minot. He addressed Fred: "If we don't go to Whitney we'll never know what great things we missed, will we?"

Fred was intent on a jackrabbit bouncing on its springs across a field of stubble. Hal did not turn back. They knew where he was going, they could always phone him. George would let him know if something came up. He didn't understand his own uneasiness. Maybe there was something in people that didn't like to be picked up and moved, even for a few days. That was old people. He wouldn't let his muscles lock and hold him in Minot the rest of his life. It was one hell of a town.

He didn't know anything about Whitney or what to expect. He soon found out. There was one street, one saloon, and one gold mine belonging to one family. The youngest son of the family had got married that morning, and the saloon was going at a pretty good pace when Hal walked in.

The bartender, a Mr. Pine, had a look of suffering as he set up glasses and emptied bottles. He had long since given up mopping the bar. He gave Hal a sour eye.

"I'm Brady. Olsen over in Minot said you needed some relief, and it looks like he was right."

The bartender slowly melted. "My God, man, get back here and start pouring. These bastards are killing me."

"I should wash up and have a bite to eat. I've been driving all day."

"You can eat when we close. Serve the judge first, he gets nasty when he has to wait too long."

"I have to bring my dog inside—I don't want him stolen."

"Sure. Put him in the back room."

Hal got Fred past a sheep dog who wanted to fight, and shut him in the storeroom. Then he went to work. The miners, mostly Finns, were giants in their build and in their thirst. You couldn't keep their glasses filled, and the noise, the smoke and the smell made Murphy's look like an ice cream parlor.

By midnight he was hungry enough to try one of the hard-boiled eggs in a glass jar on the backbar. It was not of this year's laying. At about two o'clock Pine said he couldn't take any more, and Hal could close up anytime he wanted to. He didn't say where he was going, and he got away fast.

"We're going to close now, boys," Hal announced. Nobody heard him. The judge was pretty well slopped and kept himself off the floor by gripping the edge of the bar with both elbows. When he finally let go and crumpled to the floor, two of the miners carried him to the door. "We'll be back as soon as we lock him up," they bellowed. "Don't you close."

Hal tried to get the rest of them out but they wouldn't go. He asked where the phone was.

"Hell, there ain't no phone in Whitney. What do you want a phone for?"

"To call the sheriff. I've got to close this place and go eat. I haven't had anything to eat since breakfast."

"We'll let you go eat. You go eat and come back."

"I have to lock up."

"Okay, lock up."

Hal went down the street to the cafe. There were two people at a table, a man in a suit and tie, and a woman with a fur coat over her shoulders. Not local.

The Chinaman came out of the kitchen. "We have ham and eggs. What you have?"

"It looks like ham and eggs."

"Good." The Chinaman disappeared.

"Were you at the wedding?" the woman asked Hal.

"No. I just got here this evening."

"We should have left hours ago, but I've never seen so much good liquor, I don't know where they got it. I'm over, I'm definitely over."

"Where you from?" Hal asked.

"Helena. We'd stay overnight, but the big house is running over, they're hanging from the rafters. There's no hotel, no nothing. It's the end of the earth."

The Chinaman came back with a hot platter of ham and four eggs. Hal cut into it, had the first bite in his mouth when he heard them coming up the street, shouting his name.

"My God, what is it?" the woman cried.

"I'm afraid it's some friends of mine."

The door flew open and the place was filled with boots, black hats, beards, and a heavy perfume of sweat on wool. The man got up and stood in front of his wife. "Grab your handbag, we're getting out."

The miners, not interested in them, let them squeeze through.

"Come on, Brady, we're thirsty. Open up the bar!"

"I'm going to eat my dinner. Then I'll open up."

"Don't be like that, we need a drink. You been in here eating a long time, we want you back, don't we, boys?"

The Chinaman fled to the kitchen, peeked out his little serving door. Hal took two more bites of ham, but he had no time to chew it. They gathered round, two of them took him by the arms and lifted him out of the chair, and two others poured ketchup on his head.

"Get a rope! We'll lynch the son-of-a-bitch!" A rope appeared.

Hal wished he'd brought Fred along, but then maybe they'd kill him. They hung the rope around his neck and dragged him into the street. The man and woman had got into their car but they were still there, waiting to see what happened.

"Henry, they're going to hang that poor man!" the woman cried. "Get the police!"

Hal would have told her there weren't any police if he

hadn't been otherwise occupied. The car jerked off down the street and was gone.

The crowd dragged him along the street, Hal warning them that the people in the car would be back right away with the sheriff.

"Sheriff! Hell, the sheriff's at Malta, forty miles to Malta, and the road ain't good. We'll have you swinging long before they even get there."

"Don't talk so ugly, Tom," one of the others ordered.

"Yeah, you're liable to get us in trouble, Tom. Let's just throw him in jail with the judge."

"What good's that gonna do us? The bar's still locked."

"Take his keys, he's got the keys!"

Hal didn't care about the key to the bar, he let them have it, but he tried to hang onto his own keys, especially the one to the Buick. They took everything. Then they unlocked the padlock on a tiny log building, shoved him inside.

"Here's company for you, Judge."

The judge was lying on the floor in the dark, cussing. The three windows were broken and the place was an icebox.

"When I get out of here I'll send every one of them to the pen," the judge shouted. "Ignorant, dirty, lousy sons-a-bitches."

"You're absolutely right, Judge, but let's get out of here."

"Get out? How we going to get out? They've locked us in."

When the street was quiet again, indicating the miners had probably unlocked the bar and gone in, Hal took a run at the door, hit it hard with his foot. Nothing gave way. He took another run, hit it with both feet, and the hasp squeaked. "Third time's a charm, Judge." He ran at it again, the hasp flew off, the door opened, and they were free.

"By God, I'll kill them now," the judge cried, but when he got up he fell down again.

Hal thought he'd better get the old fellow home, he'd freeze to death here on the cement floor. At the same time he was thinking of Fred. "I don't know whether to save you or my dog."

"Save me and I'll save your dog. I've got a Lüger at home."

Hal threw him over his shoulder and made his way in the dark across a vacant lot, down an alley, and up the judge's steps. He banged on the door. A small woman in a flannel nightgown appeared, leaning on a crutch.

"Here's your husband," Hal said, and dumped the judge on the floor inside.

"You've got him drunk again, Bill Watson. I've had about all I can stand from you." She reached into a table drawer, pulled out a pistol.

"Shall I take him back to jail, ma'am? That's where I found him."

"Give me that Lüger, Minnie!" The judge got to his feet and took the gun. "Make some coffee. This man is not Bill Watson. He broke down the jail door and got us both out."

She looked Hal over. "A jailbird, eh? What was he in for?"

"They threw me in for closing the bar," Hal explained. "And now I've got to go back there and save my dog."

Minnie and the judge told him that would be foolhardy, he'd get himself killed, and maybe the men didn't know the dog was in the back room and it would be all right.

The coffee smelled good in the judge's kitchen, and Minnie was getting out the remains of a venison roast for him, but he said he'd be back as soon as he could, and left. He had no trouble finding the bar, guided by the roaring jukebox, but the window to the storeroom was locked. He could hear Fred whining inside, and told him to shut up. He broke the upper pane with a rock, reached in and undid the catch, raised the sash. Fred wouldn't jump through, it was too high for him, so Hal reached in and grabbed his front paws and pulled. Fred gave a cry of pain. That was no good. Hal climbed through the window, grabbed Fred and shoved him outside, and got out again himself.

"Fred," he said, "this stuff about a dog being man's best friend is all wrong. It's the other way around." They got across the back lot. Hal, looking back, saw faces appear at the open window.

"He got out! The son-of-a-bitch got out of jail!"

Hal and Fred ran, Fred turning to growl every few yards. They got up the porch steps and into the judge's house with the mob on their heels.

"By God, they're not coming in here," Minnie cried, and gripping her crutch like a baseball bat she went after them. "Get out of here, you lousy buggers!"

The judge, grasping the Lüger, followed her. "I'll kill every damned one of you. Get off my property!"

Hal tried to take the gun. "Take it easy, Judge, this is just a joke that's gone too far. Don't shoot anybody."

"Hell, this is no joke." The judge fired. Fortunately his

aim was off, and the shell hit a cottonwood tree in the yard, but the shot riled the crowd.

"Come on, boys, let's take the old coot back to jail," somebody shouted. There was a rush for the porch. Fred bared his teeth and advanced, growling.

At that moment, a siren screamed into Whitney, with the sheriff from Malta and his deputy.

"What the hell is going on down here?" he demanded. "Can't you let a man get a night's sleep, for God's sake?"

The miners melted back. "We didn't mean nothin', Sheriff. We was just havin' a little fun with the judge."

"Where's the man you hanged?"

"We didn't hang nobody."

"You might as well come out with it now because I'm going to find out anyway. Where is he and who is he?"

"Honest, nobody got hung."

"That's not the report I got. A very respectable citizen got me out of bed and said he drove hellbent from here to Malta to get help. He saw the man with blood on his head and a rope around his neck. Now—where is he?"

"We was jokin', Sheriff. That was ketchup on his head. We never hung him, we throwed him in jail with the judge."

"I'll believe that when I see the man."

Hal had been enjoying it, and he hated to spoil the whole thing. "I'm the man, Sheriff. And I might say I'm glad to see you. Things are a little rough here for a quiet fellow from Minot."

Hal got his keys back, and then he and the sheriff and the judge went inside.

"What do you want me to do with these fellows?" the sheriff asked.

"Shoot every damned son-of-a-bitch," Minnie suggested.

The judge's proposal was about the same, so the sheriff decided to fine them all for breach of the peace and make them put new windows in the jail and furnish it with a nice comfortable cot and a chair. The windows had been out for years, and this was a good opportunity to get them in.

Hal slept in the judge's guest room, in a high walnut bed, his head on an embroidered pillow slip. Fred was allowed to stay in the room with him, not that Minnie believed in inside dogs, but she felt safer that way.

About noon along came Mr. Pine. "I hear you had a little trouble last night, Brady. I'm sorry."

"We handled it, didn't we, Judge?"

"Any bones broken?"

Hal shook his head.

"What do I owe you?"

Hal figured on the kitchen table oilcloth. Pine took out his wallet. "That's just wages. What about damages?"

"If you can forget the liquor you lost when they all went in again and helped themselves, I can forget my sore neck."

Pine counted out the money, and Hal put it in his pocket. "When do you want me to go on today?"

"You mean you'll stay?" Pine blinked.

"Why not?"

So Pine took off for two days' holiday and Hal ran the bar. There was no trouble that day—everyone was too tired or too sick. They were nursing their hangovers. By the next day they had forgotten about the celebration. Hal kept the place very dark, figuring that if the miners couldn't see each other they wouldn't get mad. If a sheepherder came in, he had to leave his dog outside. "I like dogs," Hal explained. "I have a dog. But dogs in a bar cause trouble. Somebody steps on another fellow's dog, and there's a fight. One dog is a hazard, two dogs are dynamite."

"How do you know so much about bars, Brady?" they asked.

"I was born in a bar."

"You didn't get that muscle in no bar." They all laughed.

The Finns wanted him to come out and try their baths. He did go out and watch the next morning. They got into a tent full of steam and came out and rubbed themselves with snow. It was supposed to stir up the blood. No wonder they wanted to hang people. They said it was the whiskey that made them crazy, not these good wholesome baths.

Two fellows from Haure came through and told him how Montana was honoring Mr. Volstead—it was about the way North Dakota was revering his name. Along the border there was a thriving rum-running business, spiced by the border hoppers and the Mounties. Butte, that annex to the Vatican, was so wide open the sheriff escorted the bootleggers into the city with a cavalcade of law. Kalispell, the Holy City, on the trail to Salt Lake or Butte, managed to siphon off enough Canadian for its own comfort. Every now and then some lucky fellow hit one of Louis Hill's caches of pre-1910 liquor, buried under a certain pine near a certain rock in Glacier Park, before that territory became parched federal ground.

It was all interesting, and he was getting tired of it. He had never thought he'd be homesick, but he kept thinking about Minot. He remembered Hawk diving off the top of the staircase in the Park Hotel, shouting "Green River!" Not hurt, not even bruised. Too drunk. But it was mostly Rosie he thought about.

One of the Finns was showing him a crumpled, browning photograph of his girl. "I send for her soon. When I save up the money."

"How long have you been here, Joe?"

"Ten year two month."

"You better forget that girl."

The Finn didn't listen. Hal could see Rosie waiting around ten years. He brought himself up short. He wasn't going to marry Rosie. Not on your life. He wasn't going to marry anybody. But maybe he ought to call up George or Hortense to ask if anybody had seen or heard from Rosie. Then he remembered there was no phone. Writing a letter was out of the question—he'd rather marry her than write a letter.

He began to imagine things that could be happening to her. Bad things.

The third day passed and Pine had not come back. Hal began to worry—something could have happened to keep him away for good. He was a little short with the Finns.

"You don't like us no more? You want to leave Whitney?"

"I like you fine," Hal assured them. "Only thing is, I've got a still going in Minot and I'm afraid it might blow up."

On the morning of the fourth day there was no Mr. Pine. Nobody had heard from him. The judge said maybe he had a flat tire someplace, or he ran out of money. "He'll be here one of these days. You'll see."

Hal didn't want to wait till "one of these days." He was short with Fred when he whined to get out of the back room. He slammed the change and the beer glasses on the bar.

"Maybe Mr. Pine don't come back and you got yourself a bar," the Finns suggested.

"I don't want a bar. And this bar is the last bar in the world I would want if I wanted a bar."

That evening Mr. Pine walked in. "I knew you'd hang on, Brady. I'm grateful."

"By the way, do you know Squeaky Simpson down in Minot?" Pine shook his head. "Who knew you needed a bartender?"

"Dick Scott. Railroad bull. Known him for years."

So that was it, Hal thought. Scott wanted him out of town. Maybe because of Wanda, maybe for another reason.

There was a sadness in Pine. At first Hal thought it was a natural sadness at returning to a place like Whitney, but that wasn't it. The purpose of his trip had been to see two old friends, both bootleggers. The first one, Harvey, had died as a result of his love for a country schoolteacher. The day before Christmas Harvey loaded his car with crates of oranges and sacks of candy for the kids in her school. On the way out, he wrecked his car, broke his leg, and spilled oranges all over the prairie. It was forty below zero. No one came along to save him, he couldn't walk, so he froze to death lying among the oranges. The other one, Dave, had neglected to clean the mud off his windshield, didn't see the train coming, and was destroyed.

Pine leaned his elbows on the bar. He looked much older than he had a few days ago. "It makes you think, don't it, Brady? What happens to old bootleggers?"

"The same thing that happens to old bookkeepers. They die."

11

It was late afternoon when he reached Minot, and the first person he saw was Squeaky Simpson, strolling along Central Avenue. Hal stopped.

"So Dick Scott was the one who wanted to ship me off to that bar in Whitney. How much did he pay you for making the arrangements?"

Simpson looked way off at a pink cloud over the Park Hotel. "I was only helpin' you out, Brady. But I'm glad you stopped. I got to ask you something." He swallowed. "Did Rosie Robinson have a trunk when she left your place?"

"Yes." Hal waited.

"Well, the thing is, they found a trunk with a lot of ladies' clothes in it. But maybe it ain't hers."

"Where is this trunk?"

"Down at the station."

"I'll see if it's hers."

It seemed a long way to the police station. The same solid fat man was at the desk, reading the Sunday paper. Squeaky told him Hal wanted to see the trunk, and he said, okay, let him see it, and went on reading.

It was Rosie's trunk. Hal had known all the way across

town it would be Rosie's trunk. He sat down. Squeaky stood looking at him, and his mean little eyes were not mean any more.

"Geez, Brady, it don't mean she's dead. She might of left the trunk someplace, and somebody stole it."

"Where did they find it?"

"In a field just off the highway east."

"Nothing else with it?"

Squeaky shook his head. "But they're lookin' for her now. They're really lookin'. Ain't that so, Bailey?"

The solid man didn't look up.

Hal drove out the highway east, and it was easy to see the tracks where someone had gone into a field and dragged out the trunk. He went over the ground, making a wide circle, but there was nothing more. He got into his car and drove back to town, slowly. He had to tell somebody, so he stopped at Toni Murphy's and told him. Toni tried to cheer him, saying it didn't mean something had happened to Rosie—she just got separated from her baggage, that was all.

"What'll you have? I just got some beer from Canada."

"Nothing, thanks."

Hal went on to the Prairie Dog. Hawk was there, and he said George had gone home to bed. It was pretty early for George to go to bed.

Homer came over. "Hal, some fellow called you a while ago."

"What did he want?"

"He didn't say. He just said he'd call back later."

Hal didn't like the sound of it. Why couldn't he leave a message?

One of the rails squinted across his beer. "I hear they found Rosie's trunk."

Hal didn't have to answer him, because the phone rang, and Homer said, "It's for you, Hal. I think it's the same guy."

The voice at the other end of the line was muffled. "This is something I think you want to know, Brady," it said. "They got Rose Robinson and they say if you want to find out where she is come down to the Soo Line passenger when she comes in and go to the baggage car."

"Who are you?" Hal demanded. The phone clicked. That was all. He looked at his watch. The train was due in about half an hour. He went back to the table, and Gordon McGee came in and sat with them.

"What did the guy want?" Homer asked, and Hal told them.

"You're not going, are you?" McGee asked.

"Sure."

"It could be a trap, Brady. They tell you they have Rose Robinson just to get you down there and knock you off."

Hal thought if they wanted to knock him off they could do it almost anyplace, they wouldn't have to get him down in the Soo Line yard. And maybe it was true, maybe they had Rosie down there.

"Brady, I hear you damned near got blown to hell last week. That true?"

"It's true."

"Was it an accident?"

"I don't know, McGee. I got a doped drink in the Pagoda. Maybe somebody is annoyed with me."

"You sure you didn't leave the gas turned on in your brother's flat? I hear you and your friend were up there painting all day."

Hal said he was sure he hadn't left the gas on.

"Maybe your friend did?"

"George? George is a regular old woman about things like that."

McGee gave him a funny look, but he didn't say anything. That was the beginning of a very ugly train of thought, a match to a long slow-burning fuse.

Hal took Fred and drove down to the yard. The train was in, the car knockers were checking her over, and the conductor, Red Burley, was up at the engine, talking to the brakeman, his lantern at his side.

"You stay in the car, Fred. You might get killed being a hero."

Hal walked along the platform to the baggage car. Both doors were open—that was strange, they didn't usually open the one on the far side. He peered into the car, dimly lit by the platform lights. There was a lot of baggage, but the only thing he saw was the coffin. Cold ran down his spine.

He started to climb into the car, saw a hand in a black leather glove grip the frame of the open door on the other side. He dropped out of sight, waited, looked again. No one in the car. The hand was gone. Must have seen me, he thought.

He swung into the car, bent over the coffin. It was tied with heavy rope and also sealed. He started to work on the knot, suddenly put his ear down on the lid. Breathing. Someone was breathing in there! "Rosie?" he whispered.

He heard the sound behind him too late. When he turned, a figure in a dark uniform was coming toward him, one black-gloved hand holding a gun. The platform lights hit the face of Dick Scott.

"Is Rosie in here?" Hal demanded.

Scott didn't answer, he just kept coming.

"She'll suffocate, you've got to let her out. Shoot me or do whatever you want, but let Rosie out!"

Scott was close now. What was the fellow going to do? Hal dodged, too late, caught the full weight of the gun butt on his skull.

Someone was shaking him. He opened his eyes and saw Red Burley and a car knocker.

"What happened to you, Brady?" Red demanded.

"Dick Scott hit me with the butt of his gun."

"What the hell were you doing in the baggage car?"

"Looking for Rosie."

Red looked at him the way you do the feeble-minded and the very very drunk. Hal could see he had to tell Red the whole story, from the phone call on, but first he had to see what was in the coffin. He tried to get up, didn't quite make it.

"I was bending over that casket, Red, when Scott came at me. I still don't know what's in it."

"What do you mean? You don't think Rosie—"

The car knocker untied the rope on the coffin. "Seal's broken." He lifted the lid. Hal waited.

Red went over and looked. "What do you know!"

"Well?"

"It's empty, Brady." He read the label: "Kane Mortuary, Victoria, B.C., to Martin and Coughlin, Minot." He sniffed. "It has a funny smell."

The car knocker said it smelled like the Red Pagoda.

"Chinese," Hal muttered. "Scott's been smuggling Chinks across the line. In fruit cars. This must be his new scheme." He tried again to get to his feet, made it, walked over to the open doorway on the off side, drew in a breath of cold night air. His eyes dropped to the next track.

"I been thinking Scott was up to something," Red muttered.

"He's not up to much now. Come and look."

Lying in the cinders between the rails was a long body in a dark-blue uniform, the arms flung out, the hands gloved.

Red didn't seem surprised. Neither did the car knocker. "Everybody's been expecting some poor bum in a boxcar to knock him off."

The brakeman came along. "Jesus Christ, Red, when are we gonna get out of here?"

Red looked at his watch. "We're so late now it don't make any difference, Charlie. Come here and see who finally got what was comin' to him."

Hal got back in the Buick with Fred, and sat there thinking in the blue light from the platform. Scott was dead. The message about Rosie had undoubtedly come from Scott. Who had killed him was anybody's guess, but it could have been a traveler in a boxcar. God knows he had done enough cruel things to warrant execution. But with Scott dead, who knew where Rosie was? How was he to find her now?

He drove slowly to Central Avenue. Too bad George had gone to bed. George could figure out something, he was a good thinker when he had to be. "We'll get him up," Hal decided.

George's room at the Park Hotel was empty. The bed hadn't been slept in. He must have changed his mind and decided to visit a few of his favorite spots.

Hal came a little too close to a thought he didn't want in his head. He shoved it away.

Fred barked as they passed another car with a dog in it. He seemed right at home in the Buick, taking charge of things. He hadn't missed poor old Frenchy since Hal had gone out to get him and coaxed him away from the chicken coop. Funny the dog thought Frenchy was still there, tending his underground operation.

"My God!" Hal cried. He stepped on the gas, raced through town and over the frozen ruts to Frenchy's. He jumped out and ran to the coop, with Fred after him. His flashlight fell on a row of angry hens, awakened on their perch, and a big rock resting on the cover to Frenchy's underground gin factory. He moved the rock, lifted the cover, called into the darkness below. He thought he heard a moan, but he wasn't sure—Fred was whining and fussing at his back. He went down the ladder and at the bottom located the string to a light bulb. Then he saw her, propped against a timber, her eyes closed, her skin gray. She's dead, he thought. Oh, God, Rosie. He reached out to touch her face, and her eyes opened.

He put his arms around her, and she was shaking and crying. "I'm so cold, Hal."

"You'd better drink some of this." He took the flask from his jacket pocket.

Rosie pushed it away. "What do you think I've been living on down here?"

"You do have a funny smell." He carried her to the foot of the ladder, put her on it and she slid off. He threw her over his shoulder and staggered upward. "If you do this often you'd better lose a few pounds." Outside he wrapped her in his sheepskin jacket. "Frenchy's house might be open. Shall I build a fire in the kitchen and get you warm before we start for town?"

"No. I'm afraid here. Let's get away before they come back."

She huddled against him in the car. "What made you

think of Frenchy's?" she asked. "I thought you'd never find me."

"Who grabbed you? Who dumped you in that damned hole?"

She didn't know. "Hawk took me to the bus station, with my trunk, and he left. Then they wouldn't put the trunk on the bus, they said it was too big. So this fellow standing there said he'd take me over to the depot and I could get the train, and like a damned fool I said okay and got into the car."

"What kind of a car?"

"I think it was a Ford. Black. No back seat, like a bootlegger's car."

"Was he wearing a black overcoat?" She nodded. "Where did they have you before they put you out at Frenchy's?"

"I was in a room across from the Park Hotel, Hal. I could look down on Central Avenue and see people I knew, but I couldn't get help. They watched me all the time."

"Who watched you?"

"Most of the time it was the same fellow that so kindly offered to haul my trunk to the depot. He was from Minneapolis and he didn't like tamales, that's all I know."

"He's the guy that thought I stole his boots and gun. He must have been tied in with Scott some way."

"Where's George?" Rosie asked.

"I haven't seen him since the wedding. He'll be glad to see you. He was a lot more worried than I was."

"Is that so?"

They stopped at Sullivan's to get Rosie some hot soup. McGee was there. "God, I'm glad to see you, Brady! I thought maybe they got you down in the yard, the way they got Scott."

"The tramps have nothing against me. I've been one of them, McGee."

"Do you think it was a transient that killed him?"

"Sure. Who else?"

"I guess that's a good explanation."

"But you don't believe it."

"That coffin looked like smuggling to me. Aliens, not booze."

"Sure," Hal agreed. "Chinamen. That's what Scott was up to. And I think Boots Cunningham knew it."

"So maybe Scott arranged Cunningham's accident."

That was quite possible, Hal thought.

"We have the bullet from Boots's tire. We can determine if it was fired from Scott's gun." McGee stood up. "It's been quite a night. I'm glad you found Rose."

Hal and Rosie and the dog went on up to the room.

"Where's my chair?" Rosie asked.

Hal was thinking and he didn't answer.

"In the morning I'm going up to Stanfield to see Mary. Was she worried?"

Hal again didn't answer.

"What's the matter with you?"

"Nothing. I'll take you up to Stanfield in the morning."

"Something is bothering you, Hal. Isn't it all cleared up now?"

"Sure. Everything's fine." But it wasn't fine. Something wasn't right in this picture.

In the morning Barney came by, alarmed by the exaggerated reports along Central Avenue. "You all right, Hal?"

"I'm all right. Ask Rosie if she's all right. She was a prisoner under Frenchy's chicken coop." Hal had just started to tell Barney about it when Squeaky Simpson stuck his head in.

"Ain't you up yet, Brady? I wanna hear what happened down in the Soo Line yard last night. Everybody's talking and nobody knows anything."

"Nothing much happened, Squeaky. The big news is we found Rosie."

Squeaky hadn't noticed her sitting on the other side of the bed in her negligee. "Where was you, Rosie?"

"I was kidnaped. By that fellow from Minneapolis and a friend of his."

"Come on, Rosie, they're only gangsters. Kidnaping is a different line of work entirely."

"They kidnaped her to scare me and also keep me busy," Hal told him. "Anyway, that's the way I figure it. If I was busy looking for Rosie, I wouldn't have time to find out what Scott was up to."

"What was he up to?" Squeaky inquired.

"Don't you know?"

"You're as bad as that sheriff from Stanfield. He wouldn't tell me nothin' either."

"Funny thing, though. Scott had Rosie, he figured I would be too busy looking for her to stick my nose into his business. So why does he tell you to offer me that lousy job up in Whitney?"

Squeaky thought it was just to make sure. "Maybe Scott didn't figure you'd bother much about Rosie—you were chasing his girl Wanda."

Hal looked at Rosie. "I wasn't chasing her, she was after me."

Squeaky started for the door. "Anyhow, you can bet on it no damned bum killed Scott."

"How do you figure that?" Hal was surprised.

"A bum can't afford a gun. If he has a gun he sells it or hocks it for beans." Squeaky went heavily down the stairs.

Driving up to Stanfield with Rosie, Fred between them watching everything that moved, Hal had a very comfortable feeling. This was the way it should be.

Then Rosie, looking straight ahead, said, "Hal, I had a lot of time to think things over."

"Yes?"

"I want to change my life."

He looked at her. She meant it. "You know what, honey? I haven't been feeling right for a long time myself."

She gave him a cautious glance.

"I haven't had a good fight since way last fall." He patted her knee and smiled, but she didn't smile back. "It's funny George didn't come around this morning to see you and say he was glad you were found." Rosie didn't answer. "Maybe he doesn't know yet that you are found."

A couple of miles farther on he said, "Squeaky was right."

"What about?"

"A fellow riding a freight these days wouldn't have a gun. Somebody else shot Scott."

"What of it? Stop thinking about that whole awful business, and just be glad somebody put an end to him."

When they reached Mary's house, Hal said he would go on over to the courthouse and see what the coroner had been making lately, and maybe drop in on McGee.

He walked into the sheriff's office with Fred at his

heels. McGee and a deputy were sitting there, chewing the fat. Fred started to growl as soon as he got in the door, so Hal took him back to the car. Dogs took an instant dislike to certain people—their smell or the way they combed their hair wasn't just right.

McGee said there was nothing new on last night's events and Hal went upstairs to the coroner's office.

Jay Proctor was glad to see him. "I've got a new batch, Brady. I was just wishing a fellow like you with a delicate tongue would come along." He got out his black bag with the bottles and poured Hal a water glass full.

Hal looked around the room, his eyes rested on the heavy safe with the painting of a sailing ship and morning glories. "Why does a man with a vault need a safe, Proctor?"

"Actually, I don't. But if the coroner had some business, he might want both. Especially when most of the vaults around here are open all the time so you can make coffee in them. The clerk of the court is the only one serious about her vault. She locks it up at night."

"Why?"

"Why not? She's a serious girl, our Mrs. Crane. All the court records, all the wills and estates, all the evidence from trials that the sheriff sees fit to store, to say nothing of the evidence from the bank robbery."

"What evidence?"

"I don't know. You helped him carry the stuff up there."

"Has he done anything with it?"

"Ask him." Proctor poured himself another shot. "Not bad. You better have a wee drop more, give you strength after last night."

"You heard about that?"

"Sure. Everybody heard about it."

Hal finished the wee drop. Then the idea hit him like horseradish shooting up through his nose. "Proctor," he said, "when you drink this terrible product of yours, do you get crazy ideas that seem sensible?"

"Absolutely. That's why I drink it. Once I floated off the windowsill, convinced I could fly. I broke my leg."

Hal considered his next question for a full two minutes. "Who can tell the clerk of the court to release a box of the sheriff's evidence?"

"The sheriff."

"Nobody else?"

Proctor shook his head. "Why? What are you getting at, Brady?"

Hal grinned. "Want to see a good fight? Come with me."

The deputy was gone when Hal and the coroner entered the sheriff's office. Hal began quietly. "McGee, I understand you have quite a batch of evidence from the bank fire and robbery. I wonder if I could go through that?"

McGee looked down at his hands, cleared his throat. "I'm afraid not, Hal. That's all sealed and locked up for the trial when we nail the robbers."

"I want to see that box. You can either give it to me now, or after."

"After what?"

"After the fight."

McGee was on his feet, his hand sneaking toward his gun.

"Your wife ought to sew that button on your right sleeve."

McGee had to look down at his sleeve, and when he did, Hal caught him in the belly with his fist. His gun sailed across the floor. McGee recovered, came after him. It was a pretty good fight. The coroner tilted his chair against the wall, his beady eyes bouncing with happiness. They paused for breath, and Hal had time to wish George was here, and a couple of deputies, so it could be a bigger war. McGee was getting tired. He leaned over his desk, slumped, hit the floor.

"Hey, watch it, Hal!" Proctor yelled.

Hal saw it. McGee wasn't tired, he was grabbing the gun from the floor. "We've had about enough horseplay from you, Brady. Now march back to the cells." Hal marched, shoulders sagging. McGee was shoving him toward the doorway of the first cell when Hal turned and dove for his legs, caught him around the knees. They both went down. Hal bounced McGee's head on the floor a couple of times, dragged him into the cell, locked the door, and returned to the office.

"Damn it, Proctor, I still have no order for that box."

"Just call Mrs. Crane, you say you're the sheriff, and you're sending Hal Brady up to get the box of evidence."

Hal made the call and the two of them went upstairs. Mrs. Crane had the box on the counter but she wanted a written order. Hal promised the sheriff would send that up when he had more time. Mrs. Crane still hesitated.

Proctor, through his private fog, saw a solution. "The judge can give you the order, Nellie. I'll get him."

He didn't have to, because Judge Waltham came in.

"This man wants to take the sheriff's evidence from the bank robbery, Judge. And isn't he the one they think did it?" Mrs. Crane looked deeply worried.

"All I want to do is have a look in the box," Hal told him. "And I have an idea you'd enjoy seeing the contents yourself."

At that point McGee appeared, with two deputies. "I'm arresting you, Brady, for assaulting an officer."

"Just a minute," the judge said. "Let's see what's in your box of evidence."

"Look here, Waltham, that evidence is sealed until I bring it into court. You have no right—"

The judge opened the box, and everybody leaned over to see what was in it. He pulled out a handful of hundred-dollar bills. There were a lot more. There was nothing in the box but money.

McGee had a white look around the mouth, like a kid that's been swimming too long. "It may sound strange to you, Waltham, but that's my money, out of my bank box. I was able to save it the night of the robbery, and I didn't think it would set well with some of the other depositors that I'd got my money out and they hadn't got theirs, so I just brought it up here for safekeeping."

Hal thought that was a pretty good try. "The only question now is, How did you happen to have this much money on a sheriff's salary? Could there be a slight connection with smuggling Chinks across the line, at five hundred a head maybe? You and Scott—"

"You're crazy. I'm not on the border. I had no way of pulling a scheme like that."

"Scott did the work, and you had the ideas. Like the Martin and Coughlin Funeral Home. Doesn't exist, does it? But somebody takes the coffin and releases the occupant. And somebody on the Canadian side collects the money from the Chinese who want to get across. Maybe Ah Sing at the George and Crown in Estavan." While he was saying these things, Hal was thinking that maybe now with McGee and Scott out of business, this coffin thing might be useful for transporting whiskey. He would have to look into it.

The clerk's office was becoming crowded. Somebody had spread the word that the sheriff was locked up in his own jail by a bootlegger, and that sounded like a sight worth seeing. Among those who crowded in was J. Robert Dahl.

Judge Waltham said, "Come here, Bob. Have a look in this box."

The banker looked. "Where did you get this?"

"McGee had it up here for safekeeping. He says it's his."

"May I count it?"

"Sure. Go ahead."

Dahl came out with an amazing total. McGee didn't look well. Some of the money, he said, he had rescued for friends who had boxes in the bank. They knew it was here in the courthouse. Somebody said, "Like hell they do." Dahl said maybe now people would believe him when he said he didn't rob his own bank. "I thought the sheriff got there pretty fast after the explosion. I assume you arranged the dynamite yourself, McGee?"

"From the kind of a dumb job they did, I'd say he hired that guy from Minneapolis to blow up the bank," Hal suggested.

"Why would I want to blow up the bank? Everything you're saying is ridiculous."

"I'll make a guess. You knew the bank was shaky, you were afraid Dahl would grab all he could before it failed."

McGee smiled. "Now, how could he get into my lockbox?"

Judge Waltham said it was a pretty well-known fact

that banks could open lockboxes, even though they claimed they couldn't. All four of the sheriff's deputies were there now, drinking it in. Waltham said, "Lock him up," and they took McGee away.

Rosie squeezed through the crowd to where Hal was standing against the counter. "What happened?" she whispered, and Hal said he'd tell her later.

Dahl was eyeing the boxful of cash, but Waltham handed it to Mrs. Crane. "You keep it, Alice, till we decide who it belongs to."

"What's in the box?" Rosie asked.

"A lot of cash from the bank," Hal told her. "The sheriff was putting it away for a rainy day."

"So everybody knows you didn't rob the bank?"

"That's right, honey. Now you won't have to marry a bank robber." Hal heard these words come out of his own mouth, and he was shocked.

Rosie quickly took his arm. "With the judge here, and all these witnesses, we can do it now!"

Hal felt a terrible tightness in his throat. "You can't do it just like that. You have to have a license."

"I can make out the license." Mrs. Crane opened a drawer and took out a form.

"Couldn't we get married a little bit at a time, Rosie? A few words today, a few more next month?"

"Full name, Mr. Brady?" Mrs. Crane was firm.

"I've got to call Barney. He'll want to come to our wedding."

"Full name, Mr. Brady?"

The crowd loved it. There was no escape. Hal wished George or somebody would suddenly appear to save him, but it wasn't until after the terrible words were uttered that George came puffing up the stairs with Hawkspeare.

"What's up?" he demanded. "I got a message you were in jail, Hal."

"It's a wedding," the coroner told him. "Meet the bride and groom. I'm furnishing the liquid refreshment to everybody who has a cup."

"Is it true?" George asked.

"It's true. Why didn't you get here five minutes sooner and save me?"

"Save you, hell. I'd have been your best man, and Hawk could have been flower girl."

"Sure," Hawk beamed. "I got your chair out in the truck, Rosie. You can set up housekeeping."

Mrs. Crane tasted the coroner's beverage. "Jay, you ought to be ashamed."

"I admit it's a little raw, but unless you have something better—"

"I have something better. Come with me, Mr. Brady." Hal followed her into the vault, where she pointed to three cases of bonded Canadian. "I don't know why we shouldn't all enjoy it. The sheriff brought it up here for evidence, and the jury always drinks the evidence."

There wasn't a great deal of work done in the courthouse in Stanfield that day.

Hal poured a double shot into Mrs. Crane's coffee cup. "Do you mind if we use your vault for a little private conference? We have things to talk over."

"Go ahead, Mr. Brady."

Hal and Rosie and George went into the vault. Hawk stayed outside where the liquor was.

George sat on the ladder Alice used to get at the top shelves. "When I left you last night you were going home to bed, Hal."

Hal said he hadn't made it as soon as he expected.

"Somebody phoned me to come down to the Soo Line yard so they could tell me where Rosie was—"

"And you went? My God, Hal, that was a pretty obvious trap. Who made the call?"

"Had to be McGee—he called her Rose. Nobody calls her Rose. When I got down there Scott knocked me out, and then McGee must have killed him."

"Why?" Rosie wanted to know.

"McGee and Scott were smuggling Chinese across the line at so much a head. Boots Cunningham must have discovered that McGee was in on it with Scott, and McGee could see his job and his profits and everything else in danger, so he set up the accident to get rid of Boots. Probably he'd have gotten away with it if we hadn't found the bullet in that tire, George."

"To think we handed over the bullet to McGee!"

"Not only that, but I kept asking questions about Scott —why he had money in the Stanfield bank, and what he was up to. So McGee decided to give me other things to think about. He had his helper in the black overcoat, who already didn't like me very much because of that load of alcohol, turn on the gas in Barney's flat. Then Sidney Wong doped my drink in the Red Pagoda."

"Wong must have been in on the smuggling," George added. "But these little misfortunes didn't eliminate you or smother your curiosity about what was going on."

"No, so he had that gangster from Minneapolis kidnap Rosie, and then Scott managed to send me up to Whitney to tend bar and keep me out of the way for a few days."

"Who killed Scott?" George asked.

"McGee, of course."

"Why?"

"Scott lost the cash he'd made from the smuggling

when his lockbox was destroyed. Knowing Scott, do you think he just smiled? My guess is he threatened to expose McGee if McGee didn't split with him to make up for the loss."

"So McGee shot his partner."

"Right. He figured the way to clear himself was to make me believe Scott was responsible for everything and then kill Scott. McGee put in that phone call to invite me down to the baggage car when he knew Scott would be there to open the coffin and let out the Chinaman."

"Wouldn't have spoiled anything for McGee."

"When did you know it was McGee?"

"When I was sitting in the coroner's office, inhaling that stuff he calls gin. I remembered helping the sheriff carry a bunch of stuff up here to put in this vault, just after the robbery. Where could McGee find a safer place to hide his loot than in the vault of the careful and cautious Mrs. Crane?" Hal paused. "Of course, before that, I had some pretty bad thoughts about you."

"Me?" George sat up.

"You never showed up last night."

"I was in my room, in bed."

"I looked in your room. It was empty."

"What number?"

"Eighteen."

"I'm in nineteen, you idiot."

"Don't get mad, George. When I thought about the phone call I knew it wasn't you, because he said, 'Rose Robinson,' and you never would have called Rosie 'Rose.'"

After another shot of Canadian, George forgave him. "And now, Hal Brady, what are you going to do with the next ten years of your life?"

"I'm going to be a quiet, law-abiding, home-loving husband." Hal smiled suddenly. "On the other hand, here we are close to the border, we have the Buick and Hawk's truck—Rosie, how would you like to go up to Estavan for your honeymoon?"

The three of them came out of the vault, stepped over the coroner, who was lying in a comfortable position, and made their way amidst congratulations and good wishes down the stairs.

CANCELLED

Return to any

**Edmonton
Public Librar**

service point